THE BRIDE'S HEART

BRIDES AND PROMISES

RUBY HILL

The Bride's Heart
Brides and Promises

First printing, 2018

Publisher
Love Light Faith, LLC
400 NW 7th Avenue, Unit 825
Fort Lauderdale, FL 33311

1

California 1872

Miss Hazel Stevenson smiled to herself as she sat on the porch steps, humming softly.

"Are you ready to go to the dance?"

Hazel chuckled as her younger sister, Martha, sat down on the steps beside her.

"I'm so excited."

Hazel smiled and wrapped an arm around her sister's shoulders. "Sure am. Where's John and Sophie?"

Martha shrugged, her expression a little mulish. "I don't know. Inside somewhere. Last I heard, they were talking to Mama and Papa about them coming to live out on John's ranch. Says he's got an empty cabin on his property that he wants them to live in."

Hazel blinked, a little surprised at the news. "John and Sophie want our parents to come out and live with them?" Sophie, their eldest sister, had married John Barker only a few months ago and had gone out to live with him on his ranch. It was only a few miles out of town, so they saw them often enough, but Hazel had never expected this.

"Did Mama and Papa sound as though they might agree to it?" she asked, frowning a little. "I know Papa's needing work, but I didn't think things were that bad."

Martha shook her head, her shoulders a little heavy. "I don't want to move out of town."

Hazel sighed inwardly and tried to smile. At thirteen years old, Martha was the baby of the family and a good six years younger than Hazel. She'd evidently been a surprise baby, but was dearly loved by all the family.

"I guess we have to do what's best for Papa," she slowly murmured. "I don't want to be moving away either, but he needs to bring in money somehow. Maybe helping John on his ranch is just what he needs."

"What about us?" Martha whined, twining her thick braid through her fingers. "I don't want to live outside of town."

Hazel closed her eyes, trying to convince herself that it wouldn't be so bad. "I know Martha, but it might be more fun than you expect."

There was nothing but a small sniff, and Hazel hugged her sister tightly for a moment before letting her go, trying to put a bright smile on her face. "Now, no more of that. You were all excited about the dance a moment ago, what's happened to that?" She leaned in, making Martha smile. "Is there anyone you're particularly looking forward to dancing with?"

Martha blushed and looked away, giggling as Hazel elbowed her. "No," she muttered, hiding her smile from Hazel. "Why, are you?"

Now it was Hazel's turn to blush. "No," she replied, her cheeks burning as she lied. "Not in the least." She saw Martha's narrowed gaze, the cheeky smile on her face, and couldn't help but laugh.

"Come on," she chuckled, getting to her feet and pulling

Martha up beside her. "Let's go and see if we can't hurry Papa up. The dance is sure to be starting soon!"

It took only a little bit of cajoling for the rest of the Stevenson family to make their way out of the house, although Hazel couldn't help but notice the concern on her mother's face as she left the house. She wanted desperately to stop and ask her what was going on, whether they were truly considering staying with John and Sophie, but her mother simply patted her hand and told her she'd speak about it later.

That was frustrating, of course, but Hazel soon forgot about it all the moment they stepped into the village square and saw all the dancing already going on.

Her heart lifted as she took in the view, hearing Martha's squeal of delight.

"Can I go be with my friends, Mama?" Martha asked, rushing over to cling to her mother's arm. "I'll be good, I swear it."

Her mother laughed and shooed her off, watching her youngest daughter go with a soft smile on her face.

"She is growing up so quickly," she said, half to herself, catching Hazel's attention. "Soon all of you will be grown up with families of your own."

Hazel averted her eyes as her mother looked back at her, one eyebrow lifted.

"Is that boy ever going to make his intentions clear, Hazel? Don't think I haven't noticed."

"I don't know what you mean, Mama," Hazel replied, trying to be nonchalant even though her eyes were already seeking him out amongst the crowd. "We're just friends, nothing more."

Her mother shook her head and laughed softly. "You can

keep telling yourself that, my dear, but I can see the look in your eyes whenever he comes by." Her smile grew tender as she glanced towards her husband. "It is the same look I used to have when I was courting your father."

Hazel tipped her head, looking at her mother closely. "You still love him, don't you?"

"Of course I do!" her mother exclaimed, evidently astonished by the question. "It's just that love blossoms quickly, bringing that first spark of excitement and hope. It takes time for the roots to bury down deep. That's all I meant. Your feelings will grow and change, should this be a long-lasting relationship, Hazel. Don't hurry this part of it."

Nodding slowly, Hazel thought carefully about what her mother had said, taking her words and burying them deep in her heart. Her mother was always so wise, so careful, in all that she said and did. It gave her a wonderful example to follow.

"On you go now," her mother whispered, pressing a gentle hand to Hazel's back. "I can see him waiting for you."

A sudden awareness crept over her as she looked across the square, seeing Christopher looking over at her. His eyes were dark, his face covered in flickering shadows as he leaned against one of the hay bales where some other couples were sitting. It was obvious that he didn't want to make himself too noticeable, waiting for her to spot him. What Hazel had told her mother was the absolute truth they were nothing more than friends. Although there was a spark there that could not be denied.

"He's just a little shy," Hazel explained, wondering why her hands had suddenly become so clammy. "I'd better go over and say hello, Mama."

Her mother laughed softly. "Don't you worry about me, Hazel. Go on and enjoy yourself now. I'll see you back home later."

Hazel barely heard her mother speak, wanting nothing more

than to go and speak to Christopher, wondering if he'd ask her to dance. It took her a few minutes to work her way past all the dancers who were in the middle of a two-step, but soon she made it through.

"Christopher," she said and smiled, aware that her cheeks were already warm. "Good to see you this evening."

He slowly unfolded himself, standing up tall beside her. His eyes lingered on her face for a moment before sweeping down her form. "Good to see you too, Hazel," he replied, his voice low and husky. "I was hoping you'd be coming tonight."

She smiled, a thrill of excitement racing up her spine. "Were you?"

"Sure was," he replied quietly. "You sure look pretty this evening, Hazel. The prettiest gal around, I'd say."

Her blush deepened, as she took in his tall frame, his broad shoulders, and his arms filled with strength. "You're not so bad yourself, Christopher. Truth is, I've been looking forward to seeing you." Glancing back towards her mother, who looked away hurriedly in a belated attempt to show she wasn't watching them, Hazel shook her head, laughing. "You didn't want to come over to speak to me?"

Looking away, Christopher dropped his head, evidently a little embarrassed. "I wasn't sure what your mama would think of me."

"She likes you well enough," Hazel replied, putting one hand on Christopher's arm in an attempt to push the worry from his expression. "You're a hard-working fellow by all accounts, and that's good enough for her."

His smile grew warm, as he took a step closer to her. "I'm glad to hear it." His gaze ran over her, heating her blood. "You've not got anyone to dance with yet, do you?"

"No, not yet," Hazel whispered, her throat a little dry. "I was wondering if you'd want to ask me?"

He blinked, a little surprised, before his smile grew into a broad grin. "You know what you want, don't you?"

Laughing softly, Hazel held out her hand in an open invitation. "Sure do. And I ain't afraid to go out and get it." She lifted her chin and kept his gaze, suddenly struck with a sudden fear that he might not like that about her, that he might step away and refuse to dance with her.

"An honest woman then," he murmured, looking at her steadily for a moment longer. "I think I like that." Taking her hand, he shot her a quick smile before leading her out to join the rest of the couples on the dance floor.

2

Hazel smiled to herself, as she dipped her feet into the small, winding river that ran through the dusty ground, leading towards a small copse of trees. She walked slowly through the river, enjoying the sensation. Tipping her face to the sky, she closed her eyes and drew in the sunshine, her heart practically singing with sheer contentment.

"You look beautiful."

An involuntary shriek left her mouth, as she jerked in surprise, the basket in her hand practically flying to the ground.

"Christopher!" she exclaimed, trying to pick up her basket before it began to float downstream. "Whatever are you doing here?"

He chuckled and tipped his hat back a little more, bending to pick up all the things that had fallen out of her basket. "Following you, obviously."

Her heart slowly bringing itself back down to a calmer state, Hazel rolled her eyes and laughed. "I won't believe that."

"I was out fetching one of the sheep that'd gone missing," he explained, chuckling. "It is just over there."

Hazel glanced through the trees to see Christopher's horse

standing in the shade, chewing on some small blades of grass it had found. A sheep was tethered to the horse's bridle, although it made no attempt to escape from its confines.

"It knows it was far away from home," Christopher explained, evidently seeing the surprise on Hazel's face. "Got itself stuck in some kind of brambles. Just as well I found it too, the coyotes would have been out tonight."

Hazel nodded, glancing over at him. "I'm just taking a bit of a walk," she mumbled, a little self-conscious. "I meant to be heading straight home, but this place just called to me." She looked out at the expanse of land just behind her, seeing the rolling hills far beyond her, she sighed happily and looked back at Christopher. "I'll head back soon enough."

"I'll walk with you."

Licking her lips, Hazel tried not to let her sudden burst of nerves show in her expression. "You don't have to."

Christopher looked at her steadily, his eyes never leaving hers. "What if I want to?"

Hazel couldn't help but laugh, even though her heartbeat pounded loudly in her ears. "You sure are a lot bolder out here, Christopher."

Shrugging, he reached over and caught her hand, walking alongside her as she kept walking along the riverbed. "That's cause there ain't no one out here but the two of us," he replied softly. "I don't mind telling you that I get a little self-conscious when there's other folks watching."

A sudden thought made Hazel frown, glancing up at him with a little bit of uncertainty. "Is that because you don't want anyone knowing your business?"

There was a short pause. "No, it ain't exactly that," Christopher replied slowly, his hand tightening on hers. "It's more that I ain't never felt something like this before. I guess I'm just not sure what to do with it."

Hazel's stomach tightened, the frown fading from her features. "Really?"

The corner of his mouth tipped up. "Really," he replied honestly. "I'm not going to pretend that I don't feel nothing for you, Hazel. My heart says otherwise. It's just not sure what to do about it all."

Pressing her lips together for a moment, Hazel stopped walking and held his hand tightly, forcing him to look at her. "Do you want to kiss me?" Her heart thudded wildly in her chest as she looked up at him, seeing the surprise on his face.

He scratched his head, his eyes darting away. "Well, sure. I mean, I guess so, I just thought that...."

"I'm not afraid to go after what I want, Christopher," she said quietly, coming away from the river to stand a little closer to him. "You should know that about me by now."

His hands wrapped themselves around her waist, surprising her with his sudden eagerness. "I do," he murmured, drawing her close against him. "I appreciate that about you, Hazel."

Hazel had been kissed before, once or twice, but nothing had prepared her for this. Christopher's mouth was firm and sure, his lips pressed to hers with both a gentleness that softened her heart and a fire that warmed her blood. Her fingers tangled in his hair as she kissed him back, standing on tiptoe so she might reach him better. His arms were strong, holding her tightly, his hands slowly beginning to explore her frame.

Breaking the kiss suddenly, Hazel pulled back and looked into his eyes, a flicker of worry sparking in her heart. "I think that'll be enough for just now," she murmured, hearing his ragged breathing. "I don't want to be too late, and you'd best get on back with that sheep."

Christopher did not let her go, his arms tightening just a little. "There ain't no rush." His hands began to run down the length of her body, forcing her to step away.

"There is for me," she replied, laughing softly. "Besides, some of what you're after ain't for just now. That comes after."

He frowned. "After?"

"After the wedding," she replied, aware that her cheeks were heating. "Not that I'm saying we need to think about that right now, but I won't be doing any more than kissing before then."

She saw him glance away, his own face red. Clearly, he was more than aware of what she was saying and hadn't quite found the words to deny it.

"I care about you, Christopher," she continued, reaching for his hand. "Let's take this slow. I'm not going to pretend that kissing is all I want. I think about my future and whether or not you'll be a part of it." Her worry grew as he refused to look at her, afraid that she might have already let her heart get involved with someone who didn't want the same things as she did. "Christopher? Am I scaring you off?"

His head twisted back towards her, his eyes a little wide. "No, not at all. I guess I'm just a little embarrassed by what I did. I didn't mean to be so obvious. I hope you don't think that's all I want."

Hazel let out a long breath of relief, squeezing his hand. "No, not at all. Come on, you can walk me home if you like."

He held her hand for a moment, pressing a light kiss to the back of it. "I'd like that."

Hazel smiled to herself as they walked back towards town together, her hand still in his. Something was right about this, something that felt like this could be the happiness she'd long been hoping for. As they walked, they talked together about all manner of things, from the ranch Christopher was working on, to the constant whining Hazel had to endure from Martha, simply because she wasn't able to do all the things Hazel did. Christopher laughed at that, understanding exactly what Hazel was talking about since he had four younger brothers himself.

There was a warmth in his eyes as he laughed, the slight squeeze of his hand on hers that made her smile. Hazel was truly happy.

"I suppose I'd best go now," he mumbled, as they drew near to the town. "The ranch is this way."

"And you're not quite ready for anyone to see us," Hazel finished, dropping his hand and looking up at him steadily. "There ain't nothing shameful about courting, Christopher."

"I'm not ashamed," he replied at once, coming closer to her with something like desperation in his eyes. "I can't explain it, but I'm just embarrassed, in a way. I've not felt like this before, and it's a little confusing."

Hazel drew in a breath and tried to smile. "I know," she said quietly, "but my mama already knows what's going on between us. You won't be able to hide it from people forever."

He nodded, dropping his head. "Just a little bit more time," he murmured, glancing up at her. "Just until my heart stops getting itself tangled all in knots. I want to be sure about this, Hazel. I'm not taking things lightly."

Hazel nodded slowly, beginning to understand what he meant. "Sure, Christopher. I appreciate that. Truly. I guess I'll see you around?"

"Tomorrow?"

He took her hand again, clearly worried that she was going to turn away from him without another word.

"Can you come by tomorrow? The same place?"

Her heart softened as he smiled at her, hopefully.

"Sure, tomorrow afternoon," she murmured, her heart quickening just a little. "Down by the stream."

Christopher smiled, clearly relieved as he brushed one finger down her cheek. "Thank you for understanding, Hazel. I guess I'll see you tomorrow."

"I'm already looking forward to it," Hazel whispered,

wondering if he'd kiss her again, even though they were in full view of the town.

She was not disappointed. His lips touched hers for just a moment, sparking life into her veins.

"Tomorrow," he whispered, lingering for just a moment longer before stepping away.

Over the next week, Hazel spent some time almost every afternoon in Christopher's company. They would meet at the same stream and talk together, walking hand in hand through the wild brush grasses.

Of course, Christopher would always kiss her, and Hazel would always hold back, refusing to give in to her mounting passions. With one older sister married, Hazel knew some of what went on between a married couple, for her sister had been quite clear with Hazel so that she would know what some men would want from her. Hazel, not being afraid to speak about such things, had to remind Christopher on a few occasions that anything more was for after the wedding, and he would always flush and look away, telling her just how much he respected her but how he was struggling to control what he felt.

One afternoon, when their kisses had left them both breathless, Hazel looked up into Christopher's eyes and felt her heart turn over on itself. It was a sensation she wasn't expecting, something both wonderful and frightening in equal measure.

"Is something the matter?" Christopher asked, feeling her hands tighten on his shoulders. "I didn't mean to—"

"It's not you," Hazel promised, interrupting him, her voice a little hoarse. "I guess I'm just realizing just how much I feel for you." She held his gaze, refusing to be embarrassed by what she felt. "I know we haven't exactly been courting properly and all, but you're getting into my heart, Christopher."

A slow smile spread across his face, bringing warmth to his eyes. "Really?" he murmured, putting one finger under her chin. "That's just as well, Hazel, because I think I love you."

Hazel blinked rapidly, a little surprised at his sudden revelation. Was what she felt love? What did love feel like? "Goodness," she breathed, wrapping her arms around his neck. "I don't really know what to say, Christopher."

"Don't you love me, too?"

"I—" She hesitated, the words sticking in her mouth. "I'm not sure. I don't know what this feeling really is. I guess it *could* be love." Seeing the slight frown on his face, Hazel smiled softly and tried to reassure him. "I ain't never been in love before Christopher. It's all a bit new to me."

That seemed to reassure him, and he smiled broadly, patting her shoulder gently. "That sounds fair enough to me. Now, how abouts we start courting properly then?"

Hazel's brows lifted in surprise. "You want other folks to know about us?"

He shrugged, as though it had never been much of a problem. "Sure, why not? I'm about ready for all that to happen, I reckon. What do you say to a picnic this Saturday?"

"A picnic?" Hazel repeated, her heart lifting with delight. "I'd love that, Christopher."

His lips touched hers for just a moment. "Good," he breathed, his lips brushing hers as he spoke. "I'll come by after lunch, so long as you're sure your mama and papa won't mind."

"They won't mind in the least," Hazel promised, her arms tightening a little around his neck as she kissed him back.

"HAZEL? IS THAT YOU?"

Hazel smiled as her mother walked into the room, still thrilled with what had happened with Christopher.

"Dinner is already prepared," she smiled, wrapping her arms around her mother. "I thought I'd get started on it early."

"My, my," her mother murmured, as Hazel hugged her tightly before moving back to the stove, humming to herself. "Well, something's happened to you to make you this happy. Christopher, I take it?"

Hazel blushed but nodded. There was no sense in trying to hide things from her mother.

"Christopher is coming to take me out for a picnic on Saturday," Hazel replied, twirling around the room for a moment. "Isn't that wonderful?"

Much to her surprise, her mother only gave her a small smile. "Have you checked with your father?"

"With Papa?" Hazel repeated, frowning. "Why would I need to do that? He won't care, will he?"

There was a short pause. "No, I suppose not," her mother admitted softly, "but it would still be best to let him know what's going on. He has a lot to deal with at the moment, but that doesn't mean you shouldn't let him know. He will want to know about this suitor of yours."

Hazel smiled back, feeling a little uncertain as to what was happening with her parents. "Has he still not been able to find any work?"

"Some," her mother replied, with a slight lift of her shoulders, "but nothing that's going to keep us all going. I've taken in a bit of sewing and darning but that doesn't add much."

Hazel frowned, as her mother sat down at the table,

hurrying to put the kettle on the stovetop so that she could make them both some tea.

"I know that you've been wondering what's going to happen to us, Hazel, and I should let you know now that John and Sophie came round yesterday to talk to us about their very generous offer."

Hazel sank down into a chair opposite and stared at her mother, her eyes wide. "To move out of town?"

"It's only five miles away," her mother replied, trying to sound practical although she couldn't quite hide the pain in her eyes. "We have to think of what's going to be best for us all. Your father and I have to make sure we've got enough to look after both you and Martha."

Something began to swirl in Hazel's stomach, making her face pale. "If I wasn't here, would you be able to stay in town?"

Her mother's eyes darted to hers, a shocked expression on her face. "Wasn't here? Whatever do you mean, Hazel? Don't you get any ideas of marrying that boy after you've only just started courting!"

Hearing the kettle begin to sing, Hazel got to her feet and began to make the tea, trying to calm her mother down. "No, Mama, but what if I *was* to marry. Would that make any difference?" Seeing her mother biting her lip, Hazel closed her eyes for a moment, realizing that she already had her answer.

"It doesn't matter whether you're here or not, Hazel," her mother replied eventually. "We have mouths to feed and bodies to clothe. You don't eat all that much!"

"But do *you* want to stay in town?" Hazel persisted, stirring a little milk into both of their mugs. "This can't just be about Papa."

Her mother laughed, much to Hazel's surprise. "Oh, my dear," she said and smiled, shaking her head at her daughter. "You have so much to learn about married life. Of course, this is mostly about your father. A man needs to work, and while I have my own duties, I don't go out of the house every day in order to earn. It's slowly killing him not to have anything to do."

"That's because this town is too small to give everyone a job who needs it," Hazel muttered, a slow flush burning her cheeks. "If only he hadn't fallen off that horse."

Her father had always been a hard worker, but the fall from his horse—who had spooked on seeing some wolves in the long, waving grasses of the fields—had severely injured his back. Now he couldn't work the long hours in the fields that he once had. He had tried it more than once and had come home each time in a state of agony, practically bent double to try and relieve some of the pain.

Unable to work in the fields, he'd been forced to try and find something else, but the more he looked, the more difficult it seemed to become. The town was small enough already, and there weren't exactly a lot of people that needed help.

"What about our house?" Hazel asked, drumming her fingers on the table. "We own this place, don't we?"

Her mother nodded, a flash of relief on her face. "Yes, of course we do. But the truth is, Hazel, we're going to need money to look after ourselves when we're both too old and gray to work. We can't just keep dipping into what we've saved." She shook her head, an expression of frustration and sadness on her face. "That being said, I don't want you thinking that you need to go off and find yourself a husband any time soon, just to get out from under our feet. We'll manage just fine, somehow."

Hazel swallowed, hard. She wanted to do something, *anything*, to help, but there wasn't much she was able to do. Her happiness over Christopher's plan for a picnic later on in the week slowly evaporated as she took her mother's hand, sitting in silence for a long time.

"John and Sophie are very kind," her mother said eventually, her voice hoarse with emotion. "The cabin is in good condition, and we could move in tomorrow if we wanted."

"But you don't want to," Hazel replied firmly. "That's the difference, Mama."

"John can give your father some work, and we'll have the food we need as payment," her mother answered, with a slight lift of her shoulders. "When it comes time to retire, we will have the money we need to live quietly as well as be near Sophie and, hopefully, any children she might have."

Hazel drew herself back, a little insulted. "But what about me, Mama? What about Martha? If we have children, then...?"

Much to Hazel's surprise, her mother let out a small laugh. "My dear Hazel, I am quite sure that you and Martha will find husbands of your own soon enough. While I hope you will stay in town, I can't be sure that you will. What if you decide to go live somewhere else? Start over somewhere new?" Reaching forward, she tucked an errant curl behind Hazel's ear. "Your father and I have to make decisions based on what we *know*, not what *might* happen in the future," she finished, smiling gently. "I do want you to understand, Hazel. This isn't about who we love more."

"I know, I know," Hazel replied, sighing. "I'm well aware that you and Papa love us all equally. It's just hard to think about giving up this place."

"But you'll have to do just that once you marry," her mother pointed out, her smile growing. "Don't you ever think about the future, Hazel? The home that you build won't be here. It'll be somewhere entirely different, somewhere with your husband. This house won't be your home forever."

Something like lead dropped into Hazel's stomach. There was almost a finality in her mother's voice, as though they'd already decided to leave. She didn't want to face up to that reality. She wanted things to stay exactly like they were.

"You've already chosen to leave, haven't you?" she whispered, blinking back a sudden flurry of tears. "I can tell, Mama. I can tell by your face."

There was a long pause. Her mother looked back at her calmly, her expression both grave and sympathetic.

"Oh, Hazel," she murmured, eventually. "Your father's gone out to tell John our decision. We'll be moving out to the ranch at the beginning of next month."

Ice flooded through Hazel's veins, swirling its coolness in the pit of her stomach.

"I wanted to try and talk you through it before we told you, but I guess you figured it out already," her mother continued, patting Hazel's hand. "Martha went with your father to John's ranch. She seems quite excited about the whole thing."

"We're leaving this house?" Hazel whispered, the words almost repulsive on her tongue. "We're going to live in a cabin?"

Her mother smiled, clearly not upset in the least. "The cabin is bigger than this house, Hazel, and John is busy getting it fixed up for us. You and Martha will have your own rooms, if you can believe it! John is such a kind man and so very good to us."

Getting to her feet, her tea forgotten, Hazel squeezed her eyes shut, forcing her tears back.

"Hazel?" her mother asked, clearly concerned. "I know this is a shock but—"

"I need to go out for a walk," Hazel muttered, her stomach still rolling. "Don't wait up for me, Mama. I need to go. I'm sorry."

4

G asping for breath, Hazel forced one foot in front of the other, climbing the only hill near to their town. She had to get away from everyone, just to allow herself some time to think.

There was wisdom in what her mother said, that was for sure, but it was still difficult for Hazel to accept. That house was all she had ever known. It was the place where she had grown up, the place where Martha had been born, the place where she had spent so many wonderful, happy days with her family.

"You're being ridiculous," she muttered to herself, sitting down on the grassy hilltop, looking down over the town. Her mother was right to say that Hazel would hopefully one day leave and start a home of her own. However, that would be Hazel's own choice. Right now, it felt as though the decision was being pushed on her without her consent. Her parents hadn't even discussed it with her.

"That's because they don't need to," she said aloud, trying to calm herself down. "It's not your house, is it? They expect you to be married pretty soon anyway."

Drawing in a long, deep breath, Hazel closed her eyes and

gave herself a shake. She was being foolish. What she should have said to her mother was that she would support them in whatever decision they made. After all, this was the rest of their lives they were talking about, and she probably wouldn't be a part of that for very much longer.

Not if things with Christopher continued to go as well as they were.

Leaning back, Hazel lifted her face to the sky and saw the streaks of red and orange beginning to spread their long fingers across it. The beauty of it brought a peace to her soul, calming her fractious mind.

"Hazel?"

Starting, Hazel sat up at once—only to see Christopher climbing up the hill after her, his face filled with concern.

"Christopher!" she exclaimed, astonished to see him. "Whatever are you doing here?"

"I was out for an evening's ride when I saw you racing up here as though the coyotes were after you," he said, his eyes wide as he came closer. "Is everything all right?"

Hazel nodded and got to her feet, going into his arms without hesitation. "I'm fine, really. I was just a bit upset." If she was honest, she still felt that pain, still felt that ache burning in her heart, but Hazel knew she had to just let that go.

"You're upset?" Christopher asked, cupping her chin. "About what?"

"About Mama and Papa moving to John's ranch," she replied, leaning back to look into his face as something painful stabbed at her heart. "I spoke to Mama today, and she admitted that they've made the decision. It's all happening next month."

Christopher nodded slowly, his eyes searching hers. "You don't want to move to John's ranch?"

"No, I don't'," Hazel admitted, stepping back so she could sit down where she'd been. "But now, I guess I see it from my mama's perspective. She's right when she says I ain't always going to be around and they've got to think of the future. I just wish that didn't mean having to give up a place I love so much, a place that has so many memories."

Christopher came to sit beside her, one hand around her waist as he tugged her into him. Hazel leaned her head on his shoulder, drawing strength and comfort from him.

"I'm glad you're here," she murmured quietly. "I thought I wanted to be alone, but I guess I was wrong."

Turning his head towards her, Christopher's gaze darted to her lips and, without waiting, Hazel lifted her face to his. Their kiss wasn't as brief or as hesitant as it had been before, and within a few moments, she felt her passion rising.

"I—I think I'd best get going home," she managed to say, tearing her mouth from his as she heard his ragged breathing. "It ain't right, just the two of us up here. Not alone."

Christopher didn't move, his hand tightening around her waist. "Stay."

Hazel laughed softly, shaking her head playfully. "I don't think that's a good idea, Christopher."

"Just for a few more minutes," he begged, his eyes filled with something she couldn't quite make out. "Watch the sunset with me."

It was beautiful, Hazel had to admit. Besides, so long as their kisses didn't lead to anything more, she'd be all right to stay here for a bit longer.

"Just until it goes below the horizon," she murmured, the ache in her heart slowly lessening as they sat together, her head resting back on his shoulder. "Then I need to get back to Mama. She'll be worried about me."

They sat for a long time in complete silence. Hazel couldn't help but sigh, feeling both sadness and acceptance in her soul. At least she didn't have to worry about Christopher. It wasn't as though he was going to turn her world upsides down any time soon.

"Are we still going to go on that picnic?" she asked softly, as the sun disappeared completely. "I've been really looking forward to it."

Christopher didn't answer, his eyes roving all over her as she sat looking back at him. There was heat in his gaze, something that set her blood on fire.

"Hazel," he whispered, his mouth close to hers, as he leaned forward, slowly pushing her back down onto the grass.

His mouth was hot and sweet, but as Hazel clung to him, he began to move a little further over, practically lying on top of her.

"Christopher," Hazel breathed, as he began to press kisses to her cheek and neck. "Christopher, stop."

He did not listen.

"Christopher!" Hazel exclaimed, now trying to push him away from her. "Stop, Christopher."

Lifting his head from the curve of her throat, Christopher caught her hands in his and pressed them to the earth on either side of her head. His lips had flattened into a firm line, his eyes burning her with their gaze.

"Why do you keep stopping me?" he asked, his voice low and gravelly. "I know you want this, Hazel."

"No, I don't," Hazel cried, beginning to grow a little frightened as he leaned down to kiss the curve of her throat again. "Christopher, *stop!*"

Panic swelled within her as she began to try and fight him off in earnest, suddenly terrified with what it was he was trying to do. This wasn't the Christopher she knew! He wasn't listening to her and was holding her hands with a tight grip as he moved his head lower, making her almost sick with fright.

She didn't know what was happening. She didn't know what

he was doing, or why. All she knew was that she had to get away from him before he took something she could never get back.

When he finally let go of her hands to begin pulling at the bottom of her dress, Hazel reacted. Trying to sit up, she pushed him, hard, struggling to kick her legs so that she could try and unbalance him. With a scream, she shoved at him again and again, until finally, he rolled off her body and into the dust.

Scrambling to her feet, Hazel tried to run away from him, desperate to get back home, only for him to catch her arm, his face contorted with anger.

"What are you doing, Hazel?" he shouted, grabbing her shoulders so that she was forced to look at him. "Why don't you want this?"

Tears dripped down her cheeks. "I ain't giving myself to you without a wedding ring on my finger," she cried, twisting away from him. "Don't you come near me again, Christopher!"

His hand was still on her arm, still trying to keep her next to him as she pulled and pulled to get away.

"We're meant to be together," he exclaimed, his fingers tightening on her arm. "Come on, Hazel! I've spent enough time with you for this to be the next step."

Hazel's mouth fell open, her mind screaming at her to get away. "Time? You think this is about how much *time* we spend together, Christopher?"

"Of course, it is," he said firmly, pulling her back towards him and using his strength against her. "Why else would I say I wanted to court you?"

Something died in Hazel's heart, her fists thundering on his chest as he tried to pull her tightly again him. "I cared about you, Christopher," she replied, sagging against him for just a moment as she tried to regain her strength. "I thought this was about finding a future together. About love." She looked up at him, realizing just how foolish she'd been. "That's not what you want."

He shrugged, a small smile on his face. "Maybe in the future, but right now I'm all for just exploring things. More than just kisses. Haven't you worked that out yet?"

A fierce, hot anger burst through her and, throwing herself away from him, she managed to break his hold on her arms. Picking up her heels, Hazel ran as hard as she could towards his horse.

Somehow, she managed to scramble up into the saddle, pulling on the reins, hard.

"Hazel!" he shouted, standing directly in front of the horse in an attempt to catch the horse's bridle. "Stop!"

She ignored him completely, her eyes burning with hot, stinging tears as she turned the horse around. Kicking her heels into its side, she rode hard down the trails.

The town blurred in front of her as she tried not to cry. Her skin burned from where he had kissed her, her arms painful from where he'd tried to hold her still. A deep-seated fear began to creep over her as she dashed her tears away, glancing over her shoulder as though Christopher would have somehow found another horse and come riding after her.

The sight of her parents' home made her want to scream out loud for her mama, but clamping her mouth closed, Hazel swung her leg down from the horse. She threw the reins over a post, ran inside, and slammed the door.

Her mama, papa, sisters, and brother-in-law all looked up at her, surprise on each one of their faces.

"Hazel!" her mother exclaimed, rising from her chair almost at once. "Goodness, child, what's happened to you? You're covered in dirt! Did you fall?"

Hazel couldn't find the words to say, tears beginning to stream down her cheeks. Covering her face with her hands, she felt a blanket of shame wrap itself around her, as though she was to blame in some way for what Christopher had done.

Her sisters came to stand by her, clearly distressed at how upset she was.

"I'm so sorry," Hazel whispered, as her mother rocked her gently back and forth. "I believed him. I should never have believed him."

"There's a horse outside," Martha interrupted, as Hazel's father and brother-in-law rose from the table to look.

"That would be Christopher's horse," John said slowly, looking at Hazel who hid her face against her mother's shoulder.

There was a moment of stunned silence, and as Hazel continued to sob, she felt her mother's arms tighten around her waist.

"Did he manage to...?" her mother whispered in her ear, her voice shaking. "Tell me he didn't."

Sniffing, Hazel wiped her eyes and shook her head, feeling everyone's eyes on her. "I got away," she managed to say, her legs beginning to tremble. "I don't know where he is."

Her father's eyes darkened, as he helped her sit down at the kitchen table, his jaw clenched.

"I'll be back later," he muttered, throwing a look towards his wife. "You all stay here."

Sophie, Hazel's oldest sister, looked up at her husband with a slightly stricken expression, as though afraid their father would do something they'd all come to regret.

"I'll go with him," John said at once, seeing his wife's expression. "Will you all be okay here?"

Hazel's mother continued to rub Hazel's back, nodding up at John. "We'll be just fine. You go on now. Teach that boy a lesson."

5

Two weeks later and Hazel still felt as though she were dragging her cold, lifeless heart around with her everywhere she went. Everything was cold and gray, with no beauty anywhere.

She hadn't left the house since that night with Christopher. She couldn't face going outside, knowing that most of the town knew what had happened. Her father and brother-in-law had made sure that he'd never come near her again, but in a small town, word traveled fast.

Not that any of this was her fault, or so she kept being told. None of this was to do with her. Despite the excuses that Christopher made, she'd never once led him on. He'd said to her father that she'd wanted him to make advances, that she'd wanted him to take things further, and that he'd gotten angry when she'd changed her mind. Much to Hazel's relief, her father hadn't believed a word of it.

Apparently, Christopher's own parents were outraged by what their son had done, even though he was of age to be responsible for himself. John had reported that they'd threatened to throw them out of their home should he do any such thing again, and since Christopher had nowhere else to go, he'd done nothing but work during the day and go home at night. Until he built a place for himself or found a good woman to marry, he was under his parents' authority.

But none of that could get Hazel to leave the house. She didn't want the pitying looks of the townsfolk, or to hear the sympathetic whispered words as she passed. Her shame was too great.

Running her hand along the kitchen table, Hazel found a cloth and began to carefully wipe off the table, trying to take her mind off what had happened. She'd been so foolish, believing that Christopher had really wanted to court her, really wanted to think about a future for them, only to realize that he wasn't after her heart. His shy nature had been a front, a way to get her to approach him when she might not have noticed him otherwise. Oh, she had thought him so handsome, when underneath it all, he had hoped to take something from her she was not willing to give.

Sitting down at the kitchen table, Hazel let out a long breath and tried to keep the flurry of tears at bay. She felt trapped, held captive by the four walls of the family home. Perhaps it would be good to move to the ranch. There she could start over, start again.

Idly, she picked up her father's newspaper from the table, knowing she would need to put it away. He'd obviously finished reading it over breakfast but hadn't managed to fold it up and tidy it away. With a half-smile, Hazel opened it and let her eyes drift down the page, finding very little to occupy her thoughts.

Her heart slammed into her chest, as her eyes caught on one large advertisement, followed by a few smaller ones underneath.

"Mail Order Bride wanted," she read aloud, a sudden trembling hitting her soul. Lying the paper on the table, she spread it out so that she could read it all carefully.

Hazel had always known that there were gentlemen who put advertisements in papers looking for wives, but she hadn't ever paid it much attention. She'd always thought she'd end up marrying a man from nearby, thinking that he'd be able to provide her with the home and family she wanted whilst staying close to her parents. After all, it was what most people did. Then again, circumstances had changed for her recently. This was almost an answer to her prayers, a way to let go of the agony that tied itself around her soul.

She could start over somewhere new, with a man who would treat her right—not that she could even bring herself to consider another man kissing her or taking her to bed. A lump filled her throat as she squeezed her eyes shut, trying to push away the terrifying memories.

"Maybe there's a man out there who doesn't want nothing like that," she muttered to herself, drawing in a few deep breaths as the tension slowly began to lessen. "A man who just wants a wife to take care of the home."

It was a desperate thought. Most potential husbands out there would want a wife in their beds—which she understood. Was there someone out there who didn't want that?

Frantically, Hazel pored over the advertisements, her heart slowly sinking as she read each one. They were all looking for the same thing: a wife to come live with them. However, each advertisement mentioned something like being pretty or sending a picture. It was clear what they would want from her.

The idea that had caught her slowly began to die as she continued to study the newspaper, her eyes going over almost every advertisement. The thought of leaving town had been one that had caught her off guard, bringing a sudden spark of hope to her heart, but now that began to fade away.

"New rancher looking for a wife to help support him," she murmured, pausing at one of the smallest advertisements on the page. "Cooking, cleaning, and helping with the animals. Apply...." Her lips twisted as she studied it, reading the words over and over. He hadn't asked for a picture, or even for a "pretty" wife like so many of the others. Her dwindling hope caught once more, wondering whether or not this might be the one man who would be able to help her start life over again.

Without even hesitating, Hazel got up from the table to find a piece of paper, deciding to write back immediately. After all, there might be a few women writing to him after this and she wanted to make sure he knew she was prepared to travel within a day's notice.

Her hasty note written, she sealed it and rose from the table, her heart pounding so violently that she had to steady herself for a moment. It was as if she were about to leave home this very moment, as opposed to simply writing a letter.

"What will Mama say?"

A vision of her mother's distraught face made her pause, knowing just how upset she would be over Hazel's sudden decision. The last thing she would want Hazel to do was to run away, to make Christopher's behavior the reason she left town, but Hazel could think of nothing else to do. She wanted to have the freedom to go out into the town and not feel the townsfolks eyes on her. She wanted to be able to walk the streets without people knowing what had happened to her. She would never be able to climb to the top of that hill again without recalling what had happened to her, would never be able to paddle in the stream without remembering how she'd walked alongside Christopher, hand in hand. It was as though this place was tainted for her. This was no longer the happy, carefree life she'd once had. Christopher had taken all that away.

"And now I must be the one to leave," she said aloud, trying to steady her resolve. Looking down at the letter in her hand, Hazel drew in a long breath and grabbed her shawl from the back of the chair. She hadn't left the house since the incident with Christopher, but if she asked someone else to post this for her, then they'd want to know what it was and why she was writing it.

She had to do this on her own.

Her feet almost tripped over one another as she opened the front door and hurried down the porch steps, her hands tightening on her shawl as she practically ran into town, not looking to either the right or left. Whispers followed her, sympathetic faces greeting her, but Hazel just kept walking without a word.

"I'd like to post this, please," she said as she stepped inside the mail office. "It needs to go right away."

She watched as the letter was taken from her, preparing to go on to its destination. The hope she carried began to burn fiercely as she paid for her postage, sending up a quick prayer that Stephen Grant, whoever he was, would answer her letter real soon.

"HAZEL?"

Stepping back into the house, her heart still racing, Hazel saw her mother step out from the kitchen, her eyes wide.

"I was looking for you!" her mother exclaimed, pulling her into a fierce hug. "I was worried."

"I'm fine, Mama," she murmured quietly, knowing she was going to have to tell her mother everything. "I was just posting a letter."

Her mother took her hand, still staring at her. "A letter?" she repeated, clearly worried. "A letter to whom?"

Hazel pressed her lips together and tried to smile. "I saw Papa's paper this morning." She put one hand on her mother's shoulder. "I wrote to one of the men advertising for a bride."

For a long moment, her mother simply looked at her, her cheeks slowly paling as she did so.

"I know you might think it's a terrible idea, but I have to get away from here," Hazel explained, hoping her mother would understand. "The ranch is one thing, but I'd just end up living there like a spinster for the rest of my life, too afraid to go back into town. All the places I loved just remind me of...him." She dropped her head, her emotions rising with every word. "I love you and Papa so much, but I have to make my own life somewhere else. I just hope you can understand."

A single tear trickled down her mother's cheek although a small smile tugged at her lips.

"Oh, my dear Hazel," her mother whispered, wiping away her tear. "Always so impetuous. Your free spirit has been crushed by what happened, and I know that you need to find that part of yourself again. Do you really think you have to go so far away to do it?"

Hazel swallowed the lump in her throat, her eyes filling with tears. "I do, Mama. I've written back to one of the men, and I just hope he'll be able to take me as I am. I don't want love or affection or anything like that. I just want a home of my own and a place to start over. Stephen might be the man to offer me that."

Her mother nodded, her tears now falling like rain even though she smiled brightly. "I'm going to miss you, my dear girl," she whispered, wrapping her arms around Hazel. "You do whatever you think best, Hazel. Just find a man who is going to treat you right."

"I will," Hazel promised, squeezing her mother tightly. "I love you, Mama."

6

Three weeks later and Hazel was busy helping her parents move the last of their belongings into the back of the wagon, quietly relieved that she wouldn't be living in town anymore. Finally, she'd be able to put her head outside the front door without knowing that people were still talking about her.

She'd ventured out a few times since sending that letter, but everywhere she went there was always a knowing look or a compassionate smile. One older lady had even asked her mother how Hazel was when she had been standing directly beside her.

It wasn't that she didn't appreciate their sympathy, it was just that she hated that everyone else was aware of exactly what Christopher had done. She would always feel the same wave of shame and embarrassment rush through her whenever someone shook their head or murmured something, even though she repeatedly tried to tell herself it wasn't anything to do with her.

"I think that's the last of it!" her father exclaimed, as he took a box filled with books from Hazel. "Time to say goodbye to this place."

Hazel glanced behind her at the still-open front door, her heart warring between sadness and relief. "Strange to think we won't be back here."

"It's going to secure our future, selling it on," her mother replied quietly, as tears began to trickle down her cheeks. "But I'm still heartsore over leaving it."

Hazel wrapped her arm around her mother's shoulders, holding her tightly. She couldn't imagine what it must be like for her, given that she had been in this house since she had married. All three of her daughters had been born and raised here. It held a much greater place in her mother's heart than in Hazel's.

"Come on then," her father said softly, holding out his hand towards Hazel's mother. "Let's go and take one last look."

"I'll stay here," Hazel murmured, thinking it best to leave her parents alone for a while. Smiling softly, she watched them enter the house, their arms wrapped around one another. The door closed behind them, leaving Hazel all alone.

Sighing to herself, Hazel pulled herself up into the wagon, turning her back towards the house and wanting to give them as much privacy as they needed.

"Hazel!"

A familiar voice reached her ears, making her skin crawl. Christopher appeared just in front of her, running full pelt towards her.

"Get away from me!" Hazel exclaimed, not wanting to even speak to Christopher. "I've got nothing to say to you."

The horses stamped and shook their manes, evidently aware of her uneasiness. Christopher stopped running, but still continued walking towards her, his gaze fixed on hers.

"I wanted to say I'm sorry."

Hazel turned her face away from him, her heart beating wildly in her chest.

"I mean it, Hazel. I care about you, and I just took things too far."

Snorting with derision, Hazel turned back to face him, seeing the apologetic look on his face. "You might have fooled everyone else with that façade, Christopher, but I won't be. There's not a single word of truth in that."

His expression hardened. "You've ruined my life, telling people what I did," he muttered, passing one hand through his hair. "I can't even breathe without someone watching me."

"I ain't got no sympathy for you, if that's what you're after," Hazel retorted, her fear and anger mingling together. "Get on and leave me be."

Christopher opened his mouth to say something else, only for another man to approach, his whistling jarring among the swirls of tension that surrounded them both. Hazel recognized him as Mr. Jones, who worked at the mail office. Her breath caught as she saw him holding a letter in his hand. Was it for her? She wasn't expecting anyone other than Stephen to be writing to her, and it had been a good few weeks since she'd sent her letter to him.

"Miss Hazel," Mr. Jones said, smiling up at her. "I was just on my way home when I saw this letter for you. I thought I should bring it since I know you're heading out to the ranch this evening." He glanced over at Christopher, the warm smile drifting from his face and being replaced with a look of uncertainty. "Is everything all right here?"

"Thank you," Hazel replied, taking the letter from his outstretched hand as a jolt of anxiety rattled through her heart. "You came at just the right time." With trembling hands, she opened it up, knowing that this could only be from one man. It seemed strange to be finding out about her future in front of the man who had torn apart her present.

"Christopher," Mr. Jones continued firmly. "I think you ought to be running along now, don't you?"

Christopher sniffed, turning his head away from Hazel. "I was just talking to her."

Mr. Jones put one hand on the wagon, standing close to Hazel in a gesture of protectiveness. "And I'm pretty sure Miss Hazel don't want you here, Christopher. Is that right, Miss Hazel?"

Hazel glanced up from her letter, her vision blurring. "Christopher, I don't ever want to see you again."

"Then how abouts I walk you back to your parents' house, Christopher?" Mr. Jones said, before Christopher could even open his mouth. "Good evening, Miss Hazel."

Hazel didn't even glance over at Christopher, turning her gaze on to Mr. Jones, who had a rather firm expression on his face. "Good evening, Mr. Jones. Thank you for your offer to walk Christopher home. I'd appreciate that."

"Not at all," Mr. Jones muttered, stepping towards Christopher, who was already walking away. "Take care, Miss Hazel."

Thankful that Mr. Jones had appeared when he did, Hazel drew in a shaky breath and tried to calm her nerves. First leaving their home, then Christopher, and now the letter....it was all so much to take in.

Wiping her eyes with the back of her hand, Hazel gave herself a little shake and tried to focus on the letter. She'd only got as far as the first line, the line that told her she was wanted.

"Hazel," she read out loud, focusing her blurry vision on the letter. "Thank you for writing. As I said before, I'm looking for a wife to help at home and with the animals out on the ranch. That's all I need right now. If you're still amenable, I've sent you train tickets to Thorn Creek in a month's time. I'm twenty-eight years old, tall, with brown hair. I'll be on the platform waiting for you. Yours, Stephen Grant."

The shaking in her limbs grew as she folded the letter up, her breath catching in her throat. She was free. Free to leave this town and start life over again. There would be no need to unpack her things once they got to the ranch. She could just leave her clothes, so they would be ready to go, ready to travel to Thorn Creek.

A jolt of sadness ran through her as she thought of leaving the rest of her family behind, knowing that Martha would take it worse than any of the others. They'd always been close, but life had a way of changing, of forcing you down a different path. At one time, Hazel had thought she'd marry someone from town, stay nearby, and always be close to her parents. Now, she had a train ticket that would take her farther than she'd ever been before.

"Well, that's it then."

The door of the house opened and closed. Her parents had finished saying goodbye to the house and were coming towards her. Hazel could hear her mother sniffing, clearly still upset about leaving.

"Are you all right, Hazel?" her father asked, as he helped her mother up into the wagon. "You look as though you've seen a ghost."

"Not a ghost," Hazel admitted with a shrug. "Christopher."

Her mother's hand clutched hers at once. "Christopher was here?"

"He was," Hazel replied, as her mother wrapped an arm around her shoulder. "Something about wanting to apologize."

Her father cleared his throat, moving around to ensure the horses were ready to go. "Did he touch you?" His eyes fixed on hers for a moment, his feelings on the matter more than apparent.

"No, he didn't," Hazel promised, with a small smile. "Mr. Jones came by to hand me a letter, and he took Christopher away."

Her mother's hands tightened on her shoulders. "Thank goodness he did."

"I don't believe a word of it, of course," Hazel murmured, as her father climbed up into the wagon. "He was just trying to get me to forgive him so that life would be easier for him."

Her mother nodded, her lips thin. "He shouldn't have come near you, Hazel. I'm so glad Mr. Jones was passing."

"He gave me a letter," Hazel said, as her father picked up the reins. "I'm leaving, Mama."

The slap of the reins dropping from her father's hand and hitting the board made her wince.

"When do you go?" her mother whispered, clearly trying not to cry as she looked back steadily at Hazel.

"In a month's time," Hazel replied, with a brief smile as she touched her mother's hand. "It means that I won't have to unpack any of my things."

"Leaving?" her father said, gruffly. "I know your mother talked to me about this, but I didn't think you'd be going so soon."

"I have to get away," Hazel replied, turning to look up at her father and hoping he'd understand. "Stephen has offered me a new life."

"But you don't know anything about him!" her father exclaimed, waving his hand in frustration. "I can't let you go, Hazel. He could be even worse than Christopher."

Hazel bit her lip, his concern echoing in her heart. That was true, she had to admit. The only things she knew about the man she was to marry was that he was a rancher and needed a wife. She knew nothing about his family, or about what kind of man he was.

"I guess we could make sure you have enough money to come home," her mother said softly, breaking into her thoughts. "That way, if he's not a good man, you'll have a way out."

"I still don't like it," her father interrupted, shaking his head. "It doesn't sound like a good situation for you, Hazel."

Drawing in a deep breath, Hazel paused for a moment before speaking. The last thing she wanted was for her father to put a stop to her plan to escape. "Papa, I love that you're so concerned over me, but I can't stay here any longer. I hate going out into the town, seeing everyone looking at me with their sad eyes. I hate that their whispers follow me about. Everyone knows what happened, and the more I try to put it behind me, the more they won't let me forget it. I can't keep living that way."

"But he—"

"He is someone I've never met, someone I don't know in the slightest, yes," Hazel interrupted, seeing her father's brows furrow. "But that situation has *got* to be better than this one. It's worth trying at least, ain't it? I can't stay here and let my life slowly shrink. And I know how to take care of myself, Papa. I'm able to leave again if it's not good for me." Putting one hand on his arm, she smiled up at him, her heart aching with a sudden sadness over leaving him. "You need to let me be me, Papa," she finished, her voice soft and quiet. "Besides, it's not like I am moving across the country. I will still be in California. Let me do what I need to."

Her father drew in a long breath, studying her face before dropping his head and shrugging. "It doesn't seem like I'm going to be able to stop you anyway," he muttered, putting one arm around her shoulders and pulling her close. "Then again, I've never been able to do that."

"Thank you, Papa," Hazel whispered, leaning into him. "I'll be just fine, you just wait and see."

Her mother sniffed and wiped at her eyes, a wobbly smile on

her face. "I know you will be," she murmured, as Hazel handed her father the reins. "You're a strong woman, Hazel, don't ever forget that. And make sure to write to us the moment you get there."

As the wagon began to move, leaving their home behind for the last time, Hazel looked back at it and let out a sigh of both sadness and relief. She wasn't going to be leaving this place to move into another place nearby, she was going to be leaving this town for good, ready to start over somewhere new. She just hoped that Stephen was going to be a good man who wouldn't ask her for what she couldn't give.

Her heart.

7

Hazel just couldn't stop crying. She'd already sodden three handkerchiefs and now was on her fourth and still the tears kept coming. The way Martha had clung to her, desperately begging her to stay, had torn at her soft heart. She had been so upset, so distraught, that it had pained Hazel to leave.

She'd been on the train for hours, and she still couldn't let go of the sense of loss. Her mother had been as brave as she could be, managing to give Hazel a warm, encouraging smile. Hazel's father had given her one long hug before turning away to "check on the horses". It was his way of keeping his composure, his way of pressing down his emotions. Hazel wasn't in any doubt as to how much her father loved her.

Trying desperately to dry her eyes, Hazel leaned back in her chair and tried to calm her ragged breathing. She couldn't exactly draw up to the station with puffy eyes and a red face, especially since she was most likely to get married almost the moment she stepped out of the train. She wanted to make a good first impression.

The next thing Hazel knew, she was being shaken by the

porter who informed her that they had drawn up at the station. Jerking in surprise, Hazel looked all about her and saw that the train was practically empty save for her.

"I fell asleep," she mumbled, her crashing nerves beginning to sway all about her stomach. "Are we here? Is this it?"

"Thorn Creek, miss," the porter replied with a kind smile. "Come on, now. We've already taken your luggage out."

Wishing that she'd had time to prepare herself a little better, Hazel brushed one hand over her eyes before pulling on her bonnet over her blonde curls and tying the ribbons under her chin. Pinching her cheeks, she got to her feet, straightened her skirts and made her way to the door of the train.

Barely anyone was around. Some porters were taking the last pieces of luggage out from the train into the station, but the rest of the passengers were on their way out of the station and heading towards the town. Hazel felt her breath catch in her chest as she saw a tall, dark-haired man leaning against the wall of the station, his eyes fixed on her.

Clearing her throat, Hazel tried to smile and walked forward purposefully.

"Stephen Grant?" she asked, taking in his rugged features. He was tall with dark hair, just as he had said, although there was a sternness about his face that told her he was not a man who smiled particularly often. Rather firm, if she had gauged him correctly.

He nodded, no smile of welcome on his face. "You must be Hazel."

"Yes, that's me," she replied, still trying to sound cheerful. "I'm glad to meet you."

He sniffed and stood up straight, making Hazel aware of just how tall he actually was. "Let's get on to the church then. I'll have the porters put your things in the back of the wagon, ready for when we're done."

Hazel blinked, a little taken aback by his swiftness. "We're going to the church now?"

He shrugged. "Why not? I can't exactly take you back to the ranch as an unmarried woman now, can I? Besides, ain't this what you signed up for?"

Hazel's palms grew sweaty, and she clasped them in front of her. "Of course," she murmured, trying not to be too astonished at just how quickly everything was happening. "Is it far?"

"Just up this way," he said, gesturing to a small path that led into the town. "We'll come back for the wagon."

Hazel began to walk, feeling both tired and thirsty from her long train ride. She hadn't had much to eat or drink since she'd been too busy crying her heart out, only to fall into a wretched sleep. Stephen was busy talking to the porters, which left her to walk up the path alone, giving her the first view of the town.

Much to her surprise, it looked rather the same as home, albeit a little redder. The dust and sand rolled together by her feet. As she walked, she saw an older lady sweeping the board-walk in front of the mercantile shop.

"Hi there," she greeted, wondering whether Stephen was going to be following her any time soon. "Is there somewhere nearby I can get a drink? I'm awful thirsty."

The lady's eyes grew sympathetic. "You've just come off the train?"

Hazel nodded, relieved that at least someone showed her a little consideration.

"I'm Mary," the older lady smiled, putting out one hand. "Sure is nice to meet you!"

"Hazel, ma'am"

"The church is this way," Stephen said, his harsh tone catching in her ears and sparking something like anger in Hazel's heart. Turning around, she glared at him as he came near her, seeing the irritation on his face.

He made to take her hand, only for Hazel to jerk it out of the way.

"I was just making myself acquainted with your town," Hazel replied, standing her ground. "And greeting Mary, here." She turned back to the older lady, who was looking at Stephen with something like surprise on her face.

"I was wondering, Mary, if you'd be able to tell me where I can get something to drink?" she asked again, ignoring Stephen completely. "I've been on that train for a long time, and I'm sure I might faint if I don't get something to drink soon."

Mary, however, did not look at her. Something like anger crept into her features as she gazed at Stephen, her lips thinning.

"Are you marrying this here girl, Stephen?" Mary asked, putting her hands on her hips. "A mail order bride? Is that it?"

"That's it," Stephen grated.

Mary's jaw clenched for a moment. "Then I expect you to take better care of your wife," she exclaimed, putting one hand on Hazel's arm. "For goodness sake, Stephen, she's just come off the train and you're dragging her to the church already! Did you even think about what she might need?" She turned back to Hazel, a warm smile on her face. "Now you come right on in here with me, my dear. We'll get you something to eat and drink before this brute of a man drags you off to marry him."

"The pastor's waiting!" Stephen exclaimed, only for Mary to go rigid and spin on her heel back towards him.

"Then the pastor can wait a little longer!" she cried. "And so can you."

Hazel, a little stunned by all that had taken place, managed to follow Mary inside, a little worried about her husband-to-be's character. She patted her pocket self-consciously, fully aware that she had the money inside, should she need to go back home.

"Now," Mary said, as she led Hazel to the back of the shop. "You just sit yourself down here and I'll get you a few things."

Hazel, sitting down on an old rocking chair that sounded as though it would splinter beneath her at any moment, smiled as Mary handed her an apple and a glass of water, before putting down a tray of freshly made cookies on the table between them.

"Thank you ever so much," Hazel murmured, before drinking thirstily. "You're very kind."

"We take care of people round these parts," Mary replied, with a firm look in her eye. "Now are you sure you want to be marrying that man? Stephen Grant ain't known for being the pleasantest of men."

A stone dropped in Hazel's stomach. "Are you saying he's cruel?" She shuddered, her free hand gripping the arm of the chair. "I've been bullied by a man before, and I ain't going to let that happen again. I'd rather turn around and get back on that train before I tie myself to that kind of man."

Mary tilted her head and studied Hazel for a moment. "You're a strong woman then?"

Recalling everything that had happened with Christopher, Hazel shrugged. "I'm not sure I am," she replied honestly. "I used to be, but then..." Closing her eyes, she tried to smile. "The only reason I'm marrying Stephen is to get away." She opened her eyes and shook her head. "That's not exactly strong, is it?"

Mary's expression grew sympathetic. "It's a way out though. There ain't no shame in taking it if things are getting too hard." Letting out a long breath, she folded her hands in her lap and looked directly at Hazel. "Listen, Stephen Grant ain't a bad man. He's not cruel, and he won't hurt you, not ever. He's got a good heart underneath those layers of ice."

"He looks like a man who doesn't have a lot of happiness," Hazel replied quietly, munching her apple. "Did something happen to him?"

Mary put a finger to her lips and shook her head, her eyes smiling. "That would be for him to tell you, if he ever does." Her shoulders slumped, as she looked over at Hazel. "He's not going to be able to love you though. Are you sure this is a marriage you want to go into?"

Hazel let out a choked laugh, startling Mary. "Then if that's all that's worrying you, you don't need to concern yourself with that any longer. I'm not looking for that kind of thing either."

"You're not?" Mary asked, surprised. "I thought most mail order brides hoped for that at some point."

"Not me," Hazel replied emphatically. "And, if things don't work out, I've got enough money to take me back home."

"And you can always come talk to me," Mary replied firmly, as Hazel got to her feet, feeling much more refreshed. "I'm sure I'll be seeing a lot of you."

Hazel smiled, feeling as though she had already made a good friend in this new town. "I sure appreciate your hospitality, Mary. I'd best be getting on now."

Mary smiled, and much to Hazel's surprise, threw her arms around her and hugged her tight. Her gesture was so much of a surprise that Hazel found tears come into her eyes almost at once, her heart aching just a little.

"Welcome to Thorn Creek," Mary murmured, finally releasing her. "You're going to do just fine out here, I know it. Stephen needs a strong, bold woman like you. Just don't let yourself be afraid of his gruff nature."

Hazel lifted her chin, blinking back her tears. "Don't worry, I won't," she replied firmly. "Thank you, Mary."

Stephen Grant paced up and down outside the mercantile, already frustrated with the situation. Sure, he hadn't cared much for anything other than getting to the church, but that hadn't meant he'd not thought of getting Hazel something to eat or drink after that. The truth was, he was now worried that whatever Mary had to say about him, it would put Hazel right off wedding him—and he *needed* a wife.

Life was slowly beginning to get on top of him, and he struggled to cope. Not that he'd admit that to anyone, mind you, since that would be showing some kind of weakness—a weakness he refused to talk about.

He'd bought a ranch only a few months ago, thanks to money his papa had left him when he'd passed. It had been something Stephen had dreamed of for years, and now that he had it, he was only just beginning to realize just how difficult things really were, trying to run a ranch practically single handed.

Of course, he had two men to help him, Joe and Ned, but they slept in the cabin while he stayed in the house. It didn't afford him a lot of company, especially since he was the owner and they were just the hired workers. Not that they weren't friendly enough, but there was clearly some kind of distance between them.

Getting up to run his ranch, as well as cook all his own meals, clean all his own clothes, and even try his hand at darning had left him exhausted. He wasn't looking for someone to warm his bed or give him sweet kisses when he came in from the ranch, but rather a wife who was able to run the house while he ran the ranch. Almost like a partnership of sorts, he supposed.

And now, Hazel had arrived. She was prettier than he had expected, with dark brown eyes, blonde curly hair, and a dusting of freckles over the bridge of her nose. She looked robust enough, although he couldn't help but be frustrated with how she'd gone off on her own to introduce herself to Mary instead of waiting for him to show her the way to the church. He just had to hope that this display of tenacity was just a brief moment of stubbornness. The last thing he wanted was a dogged, persistent wife who wouldn't do as she was told.

"READY?"

Spinning around, Stephen saw Hazel framed in the doorway, her eyes fixed on his.

"Yes, of course," he muttered, passing a hand over his eyes in relief. "Are you feeling better?"

"How nice of you to ask," she replied, with just a hint of mockery. "Much better, thank you."

His cheeks burned as he became aware of just how much he'd already failed in her eyes. "The church is this way," he muttered, gesturing in the opposite direction. "So long as you're still amenable."

For a moment, he thought Hazel was going to refuse him, but much to his relief, she simply shrugged and kept on walking. Apparently, Mary hadn't said too much against him, which he was grateful for. There was a lot more to his story than Hazel knew, but the chances were he'd never want to talk to her about it.

He never wanted to talk to anyone about it.

"Are you ready to do this?" he asked, wondering whether or not he should take her hand. "I know this is a lot to take in, being awful quick and all."

"Yes, it is rather," she replied, looking up at him. "I'm gonna tell you now that I've got parents waiting to hear from me back home. If they don't, my papa is going to be on the train here to find me. No doubt about it." Her eyes flashed with an inner fire, her chin lifted.

"I'm not going to hurt you," Stephen replied, a little affronted that she would think so little of him. "I'll be as good a husband as anyone—just without any of kind of affection." He glanced at her, worrying that she might have secretly been hoping for such a thing.

She tossed her head. "I'm glad to hear it, Stephen. You'll find me hardworking, honest, and blunt." Glancing over at him, she gave him a small smile. "I hope you're prepared for all that."

Stephen cleared his throat, rather relieved that they were approaching the church. "The pastor's expecting us," he mumbled, holding open the door for her. "Just go on in."

There was no hesitation on her part. Instead, she walked straight in, and within a few moments, greeted the pastor with a warm smile.

"So you're to be Stephen's wife, are you?" the pastor asked, glancing over at Stephen. "I'm quite sure you're going to live wonderfully together. Any problems, however, you know where I am."

"I'm sure we'll be just fine," Hazel replied, walking up to the front of the church. "Is this where I should stand?"

Stephen paused, as the pastor made his way forward, making Hazel stand just in front of his pulpit. He looked over at his wife-to-be, suddenly filled with doubts over his decision to write for a mail order bride. Hazel had been the first response he'd received, and since he wasn't sure he'd get any others, he'd written back to her straight away. Was he really willing just to tie himself to a veritable stranger, just so he could get some help on his ranch?

"Are you coming, Stephen?"

Her voice was crisp, her eyes clear, as she looked over at him with one raised eyebrow. The pastor was also waiting for him, looking a little impatient. It wasn't as though he now had any choice in the matter. She'd come all this way on the promise that he'd wed her, and that was exactly what he planned to do. It had all seemed so simple, right up until he reached this very moment, the moment he'd have to give his vows and promise himself to her for the rest of his days.

"Stephen, either you're doing this or I'm getting back on that train," Hazel said a little louder. "I ain't going to be waiting here all day for you to make that decision."

He swallowed and bowed his head, not wanting to show her any kind of weakness.

"I was just thinking," he muttered to her, his legs feeling like heavy sacks of grain as he walked into the church. "Sorry. Of course, we're doing this. Carry on, Pastor."

His heart began to pound in his chest as the pastor began to speak. He hadn't thought he'd find this so difficult.

Memories began to flood his mind, memories of the last time he'd stood up in this church. His breathing quickened, forcing him to drop his head and concentrate on simply getting through this. Giving himself a slight shake, he pushed his thoughts away, listening only to the sound of his breath. The pastor's voice faded into the background. The painful stings of the past slowly began to fade. Finally, he managed to take control.

"Stephen?"

Jerking his head up, he saw Hazel looking at him, one eyebrow raised and a slight look of frustration on her face. Clearing his throat, he glanced at the pastor, who was also looking at him in much the same way.

"Sorry," he mumbled, feeling hugely embarrassed. "What did you say?"

Hazel let out a frustrated breath. "Do you want to marry me or not?"

"I do," Stephen replied, without a moment of hesitation, determined to get through this. "Sorry, I was—"

"And will you take this man to be your lawful wedded husband?" the pastor interrupted, looking over at Hazel.

Her eyes fastened on his, and just for a second, she didn't answer. Stephen looked back at her, forcing himself not to look away. He'd made a mess of this so far, and he had to reassure her that this was what he wanted, that he'd be as good a husband as he could be.

"I do," came her whispered reply, her eyes dimming just a little.

The pastor smiled and then announced them husband and wife before praying a blessing over them both.

Stephen couldn't close his eyes, couldn't look away from the woman standing in front of him. The expression on her face had been one of sadness, as though she was suddenly torn apart by what she was doing. To his shame, Stephen realized he barely knew anything about her family, or her background. All he'd really cared about was whether she would be the kind of wife he needed. Was she sad about leaving her family behind?

Had she been given no other choice but to find herself a husband?

"You may now kiss the bride."

Those words hit him hard, his questions about his new wife evaporating in an instant. She looked at him with clear expectation, waiting for him to do just what the pastor said.

It was too close, too personal. He couldn't touch his lips to hers, not when he'd promised her there would be nothing of the kind between them. If he kissed her now, then he might remember what it felt like, and in his dark moments, long for it again. He wasn't about to fall into that trap, not for the second time.

Hearing the pastor let out a long breath, clearly getting rather annoyed with Stephen for taking up so much of his time, Stephen leaned forward and brushed his lips against her soft cheek, one hand on her waist. He could feel her tensing as he did so, her body going almost rigid. There was no jerking of his heart, no warmth rushing into his veins, just a calm acceptance that he was now a married man. Married to a woman who would share his home and his life, but not his heart.

When he stepped back, he expected to see something like confusion or even upset on his bride's face. Much to his surprise, she looked rather relieved. Her eyes were on the pastor as he finished, a small smile settling on her face as she slowly began to relax.

"Right then, I expect we'll see you both again on Sunday," the pastor said, sticking out his hand and shaking Hazel's one firmly. "Wonderful to have you join our little town, Mrs. Grant."

Hazel paused, her smile fading. "Just 'Hazel' will be fine, pastor. I'm not one for formal titles."

The pastor chuckled, an understanding look on his face. "It'll all take a bit of getting used to, Hazel, but it'll come in time. I'm sure Stephen here will make certain you've got everything you need to settle in." He threw Stephen a sharp look, as though warning him that he himself would be keeping a firm eye on Stephen's new bride. "And, when you come back on Sunday, I'm sure Stephen will be delighted to have you meet some of our townsfolk. The women have a quilting circle that meets once a week, in the evenings."

"She won't be able to join that," Stephen interrupted gruffly. "The ranch is going to be busy and—"

"That sounds wonderful, Pastor," Hazel said loudly, stepping a little in front of him. "I'd love to join the quilting circle. Everyone needs friends, don't they? That sounds like a wonderful way to make some new ones of my own."

A jagged anger sliced through Stephen's heart, his hands clenching as the pastor smiled and agreed with Hazel, not questioning her over her direct disagreement with her husband. As far as Stephen was concerned, his wife's place was on the ranch, not galivanting all about town for something as foolish as the quilting circle. Besides, she wasn't going to need friends, not when she had to take care of him and their home.

"We'd best be going," he said, putting one hand on his wife's arm. "The wagon will be ready to go by now, and I'm sure you're going to want to get home and get rested before you start on dinner."

Hazel turned around slowly, her eyes fixed on his. "Dinner?" she repeated, looking at him in confusion. "You want me to make dinner the first night I've come to live with you?"

Stephen shrugged, not understanding her frustration. "Sure. I mean, that's what wives do."

The pastor stepped forward, putting himself directly between them both. "I know that Mrs. Lawrence makes the most delicious pies you've ever tasted—meat pies and apple pies," he said quietly, looking over at Hazel. "Why not get yourself a couple?"

Hazel lifted her chin, looking over at Stephen with a chill in her gaze. "That sounds just wonderful, Pastor," she replied, her lips thinning as she glared at Stephen. "After all, I'm going to need a little time to get myself settled in and *rested* after what was a rather long journey."

"Of course," the pastor agreed, turning his own gaze onto Stephen. "You're both going to need to start looking out for each other, now that you're married. And that starts with pies for dinner, so your wife doesn't have to cook."

A flush of heat rippled up Stephen's chest and into his face, making him fully aware of just how he'd failed, yet again.

"Sure thing," he muttered, picking up his hat and jamming it on his head. "Thank you, Pastor. Come on, Hazel. Time to go home."

9

Hazel tried her best to hide her nerves as Stephen lifted her down from the wagon. There was something terrifying about leaning into his arms, feeling the strength of them as she held onto him tightly. The moment her feet hit the ground, she backed away, desperate for him to drop his hands from her waist.

Thankfully, he seemed just as unwilling to hold onto her, which Hazel couldn't help but be relieved about. Giving him a tight smile, she looked over his shoulder towards the house, taking in the large, stone chimney.

"This here is our home," Stephen said, lifting his chin in the direction of the house. "The cabin over there is where Joe and Ned sleep, and there's a creek running just behind the house."

"Joe and Ned?" Hazel repeated, wondering why he hadn't mentioned them before. "Are they your brothers?"

He snorted and shook his head. "I ain't got no brothers," he replied, with a wry smile. "Got a sister though. She's married and moved away. My parents are gone, and I'm the only one left in these parts. Ned and Joe work for me. They get food and a place to sleep, with a small monetary sum to go along with it."

Hazel nodded, trying to ignore the small curl of fear in her belly at the thought of being so close to three different men. "They don't come in the house?"

Stephen frowned, looking at her with a slightly puzzled expression. "No, they don't. That place is mine and no one else's. A man has gotta have respect from his workers. So, no, they don't come into my property. Not unless I invite them."

Letting out a long breath, Hazel tried to smile despite the worry climbing all through her. "I understand."

He paused, his eyes on hers. "You don't have to worry about them, Hazel."

Hating that her fear was so transparent, Hazel lifted her chin and held his gaze. "I ain't afraid."

Tilting his head, Stephen looked back at her, something flickering in his eyes. "Okay. Whatever you say."

Turning around so that she didn't have to face him any longer, Hazel took in her new home.

"There's the barn, and that there is the corral," he continued, pointing towards the large fenced area just across from the house. "The cattle are out on the plains at the moment, so I head on out there most days."

Hazel nodded, her hands on her hips. "I can see you've got a snubbing post there," she said, walking a little closer to the corral. "Do you tame horses too?"

The surprise on his face told her that he hadn't been expecting her to notice something like that.

"Sure do," he said, with a small smile. "I don't take them from the plains—those beasts are meant to be free—but I take the ones that no one else has the time for. The ones who are stubborn and determined." He lifted one eyebrow and smiled at Hazel, his whole appearance changing in that moment. "They usually come around in the end."

Hazel's stomach tightened, making it hard to breathe.

Stephen's expression had brightened entirely, changing from a sullen, frustrated man to one who looked as though he had every happiness in the world right at his feet. The smile touched his eyes, making his green eyes almost sparkle in the sunshine. She couldn't look away.

"I didn't know you knew much about horses," he continued, as they walked towards the corral. "I'm guessing you know how to ride, but apart from that—"

"My brother-in-law owns a ranch," Hazel explained, as she leaned on the corral fence. "He breaks horses in sometimes. I've watched him do it." A small smile touched her mouth as she saw the two horses in the corral begin to come towards them, evidently looking for something to eat. "They're beautiful," she murmured, as a small grey mare came towards her, whinnying gently.

"My goodness," Stephen whispered, as Hazel held out her hand to the mare. "Now ain't that something."

Confused, Hazel looked over at him, taking the proffered sugar cube he held out to her.

"I keep a few of these in my pocket most of the time," he explained, as she gave it to the mare. "But that mare there, she is one of the shyest creatures I've ever known."

"Shy?" Hazel laughed, making the mare dance away for a moment. "I wouldn't say she's shy." She smiled gently, as the mare let her stroke her quivering neck for a moment, before snuffling for more sugar.

Stephen cleared his throat, still evidently rather surprised. "That's just what I mean, Hazel," he said quietly. "She's never come near me the way she's approached you. She runs away from me most of the time, and it's difficult even getting near her!"

"Maybe she and I share a kindred spirit," Hazel murmured, as the horse came a few steps closer. "What's her name?"

He shrugged. "She ain't got one." Stepping away from her, he paused for a moment. "How abouts you name her for me? I'll get the rest of the luggage inside. Come in when you're ready."

Hazel didn't look behind her as Stephen moved away, her heart filled with a small, flickering happiness that hid all her concerns and worries for a moment. The mare seemed to understand her sense of being a little afraid, which was maybe why she was so willing to come close to Hazel.

"We're going to get along just fine," Hazel whispered, as the mare sniffed her hand again before turning away when she didn't find any more sugar. "I'm not sure what to call you yet, but I'll think of a good name, don't worry." She smiled to herself, as she leaned on the fence, watching the two horses walk together to the other side of the corral.

Turning around, she took in her new home. It was bigger than she had expected, with a large barn to one side and her house on the other. The news that there were two other men living beside the house had been something of a shock, making her wonder whether or not she'd really be safe when Stephen went out to the cattle every day. Of course, most likely, they'd go out with Stephen too, but she still didn't like the idea of being there alone.

Although it didn't look like she'd have much of a choice.

Swallowing the worry that began to rise in her again, Hazel made her way back up to the house, aware that Stephen was busy putting the horse and wagon into the barn. She'd have a few minutes to herself to take in her new home.

Climbing the porch steps, Hazel paused for a moment, her hand on the door latch. This was it. Finally, this place was to be her home, a place she could make her own. It was going to take a lot of work, but in time, Hazel was sure it would feel like home. Just so long as Stephen was good-natured, she was quite sure it wouldn't be too long until she settled in.

Taking in a deep breath, Hazel opened the door and stepped inside, her heart in her throat. Looking all about her, her footsteps echoing on the wooden floor, she took it all in.

There was one large room with a fireplace and stove connected to the stone chimney. The house would be warm enough at night, that was for sure! The water basin was next to that, alongside the kitchen table and chairs. Hazel ran her hand over the table, wondering if it was something Stephen had made himself. Moving through the rest of the house, she saw another room next to the staircase, and climbing the stairs, she found another two bedrooms and a smaller box room. Everything was very neat and tidy, as though carefully organized. She was a little afraid to move something, feeling as though it might make Stephen angry if she did so.

Pushing down that feeling, Hazel continued to look around the house, her heart slowly filling with happiness. Shaking her head to herself, she wrapped her arms around her waist and hugged herself with delight. This was bigger than any home she'd ever been in, filled with space and light. It would be a wonderful place to call home.

"Are you in here, Hazel?"

"Just coming down," she called back, still smiling as she walked down the stairs. "Your house is lovely, Stephen."

He didn't look up from what he was doing, busy setting out the pies on the table. "You can have either of the rooms up the stairs," he said rather gruffly. "I sleep in there." He jerked his head towards the room by the staircase, the one she'd not really looked into. "I'd prefer my wife be upstairs at night, just to be safe."

Hazel frowned, something like fear clutching at her stomach. "Are there bandits around these parts?"

Pausing in what he was doing, Stephen looked up at her, straightening up to face her. "No, not really, but a ranch owner can never be too careful. I've got a lot of decent cattle and horses here. Best you stay upstairs."

Understanding what he meant, Hazel tried to smile, her happiness beginning to blow away. "I'll take my things up then."

"I can do that for you," came the hurried reply. "You need to rest."

Hazel ignored him and picked up one of her bags, leaving him to get the rest. Climbing the stairs, she poked her head into the two largest rooms before settling on the one that looked out over the ranch. She'd be able to see the horses from her bedroom.

"This one will do just fine," she said, setting her bag down. The room was well furnished, with a wardrobe, drawers, and a cozy-looking bed, but there were no drapes on the window and certainly no homey touches. Not that Hazel minded that, she'd be able to set most things right soon enough.

"Fine," Stephen muttered, his breath coming rather quickly as he put down the rest of her things in her room. "You won't be disturbed here, I promise you that."

Hazel turned to face him, keeping her gaze steady. "I'm well aware that you don't want any kind of affection between us, Stephen."

He nodded, his cheeks burning with color as his gaze darted away. "And are you sure you ain't going to want that?"

A ripple of laughter escaped from Hazel's throat, clearly surprising him. "I can promise you, Stephen, that I won't be looking for anything of the kind." She laughed all the more at the astonishment on his face, realizing that he evidently believed most women sought that kind of thing in their marriages.

After a moment or two of quiet, Stephen cleared his throat and shrugged. "Well, good we've got that sorted out. I'd best get back down to put the horses away. Ned and Joe will be back from the pastures soon enough. They were out looking after the cattle today, and I'll be heading out with them first thing tomorrow morning." He looked at her steadily for a moment, his expression a little uncomfortable. "Do you think you'll be all right to make breakfast?"

Hazel couldn't help but grin. "So long as you show me where the hen house is, I'll be more than willing to do that."

A look of relief crossed his face. The man wasn't much of a cook, perhaps.

"I'll leave you to unpack," he muttered, turning away. "Those pies need to be warmed for dinner, but that's all."

"I'll see to it," Hazel replied, looking around at her things and mentally beginning to unpack everything into various spaces. "In about an hour?"

"An hour is just fine," came the reply. "Thank you, Hazel."

10

The first night at the ranch had not been easy. Hazel had barely slept, her mind whirling with all that had happened, even though her bones were weary with exhaustion. The ranch had lots of different sounds compared to her home in town, especially at night. Coyotes howled in the moonlight while other night creatures scuffled across the sand. At one point in the night, Hazel had risen from her bed and gone to look out of the window, seeing the moon spreading its light across the ranch. It looked both ghostly and wonderful at the same time.

She had returned to bed and fallen into a rather restless sleep, struggling to find peace. She had woken numerous times, confused and disorientated, before finally falling into a deep sleep only a few hours before sunrise.

The change in the light had been what had woken her. Pushing herself up on her elbows, Hazel looked out at her room, her heart thundering in her chest. Was she late? Had Stephen already left?

Dressing quickly, Hazel grabbed her apron and tied it around her waist before hurrying to the door. Quick fingers retied her long hair into a neater braid as she made her way down the stairs, her bare feet growing cool on the wooden floorboards. Stephen's room still had its door closed, which had to be a good sign.

Letting out a sigh of relief, Hazel saw that he wasn't about and quickly set to making breakfast. Luckily, Stephen had shown her where he stored everything, including the meat. It didn't take her long to have the bacon and beans ready, adding some scrambled eggs to go with it.

Mentally kicking herself for not having left bread to rise overnight, Hazel set out what she would need to make bread later that day and quickly made a dough for biscuits. They were added to Stephen's breakfast plate and *still*, he hadn't appeared.

The coffee was made. The food was ready. The table was laid.

Not quite sure what to do, Hazel hesitantly made her way to Stephen's room, knocking gently on the door.

The sound of barking from inside the room made her start with surprise, stumbling back a little.

"Be quiet, will you?"

The door opened and Stephen, looking half asleep, stood in the doorway rubbing his eyes. "What's the matter?"

Hazel pressed her lips together for a moment, not quite sure where to look. Her husband was standing at the door with nothing on but his breeches, having clearly just woken up.

"I've made breakfast, and it's going to grow cold if you don't come and eat," she managed to say, keeping her gaze averted. "And I didn't know we had a dog."

He grunted, turning around to look out of the window behind him. Hazel saw him stiffen, before turning around to face her, his eyes widening. "How long have you been awake?"

"Not long," she replied, seeing his eyes close with either relief or frustration. "What about your breakfast?"

He groaned and shook his head, walking back to his bedroom but leaving the door open. "I'll be there in a minute," he called, as a large collie came out of the room and came straight towards Hazel. "I'll not be long. I think I'm already late. Can you feed Max?"

Hazel didn't quite know what to say, turning around and walking back into the kitchen with the dog at her heels. Her mouth was inexplicably dry, the palms of her hands sweating as she went to wash them. Max barked once, making her jump. She had no idea what to feed him or where to find the food. Forcing herself not to think about the state she'd seen Stephen in, Hazel tried to find where Max's bowl was kept.

By the time she'd done that, Stephen was sitting down at the table, looking as though he'd never seen such a sumptuous meal in his life. He said grace and began to eat, throwing her a wide smile as he took a bite of one of his biscuits.

"Thank you, Hazel," he said, chewing loudly. "I ain't had as good a breakfast as this in years."

"You're welcome," Hazel replied, turning back to the stove, so she could start making her own breakfast. "I'm sorry you're late."

He shrugged. "I'm not late yet. I can eat fast." His eyes turned to hers again, fixing her with his gaze. "Thank you for waking me. I must have been tired after all that happened yesterday."

Hazel found herself blushing but could not account for it. She kept her back to him, while focusing on cooking the eggs. "When will you be back?"

"In time for dinner," he replied, wiping his mouth. "You gonna be okay here by yourself?"

Scooping up the eggs to put on her own plate, Hazel nodded. "I'll be just fine," she replied, sitting down across from him. "I got plenty to do around this place."

"I know there's all manner of things you're going to need

from town, but I'll take you later this week, when I'm not out to pasture. Just see if you can make things stretch, will you?"

Hazel bit her lip, keeping back her harsh retort that she could manage to go to town all on her own. He clearly had expectations, and their first morning together wasn't the time to start questioning them.

Stephen got up practically the moment she sat down, throwing back the rest of his coffee in one gulp. "I'd best be going," he said, wiping his mouth with the back of his hand. "The others will be waiting for me." He lifted one eyebrow and paused for a moment. "Are you sure you're going to be all right here?"

"Yes, I'm sure," Hazel replied, a little frustrated that he didn't seem to believe her that she could manage on her own. That was the second time he had asked her. "I'm not about to get all lonesome just because you're not around." Her sharp words seemed to surprise him, his eyes widening just a little, before he turned around and walked straight out of the house without even wishing her goodbye.

Hazel blew out a frustrated breath, not sure whether she was more annoyed with him or with herself. He was trying to be kind to her, she supposed, but she was more than capable of managing things on her own. Besides, she was going to have to get used to being here by herself.

As much as she hated to admit it, Hazel felt a little spooked being in this big house all alone. Whether it was because it was just a brand-new situation, or because of all she'd been through, she wasn't sure. Her skin prickled as something creaked upstairs, even though she knew it was just one of the noises that came from a house like this.

Since her breakfast was finished, she made her way to the porch. She opened the door and stepped out into the morning sunshine, coffee cup in hand. She'd spend a few minutes praying, simply enjoying being in a new place and a new situation, before heading back inside and carrying on with all the things she had to do.

Stephen came riding out of the barn, two men on horseback coming to join him. She supposed they were Ned and Joe, Stephen's workers. They were heading towards the house, which would lead out to the pastures. Even though something like nerves rolled in her stomach, she stayed exactly where she was.

The horses drew up alongside the house, and Hazel tipped her face up towards them, squinting a little in the sunlight.

"This here is my wife," Stephen grunted, not looking at her. "Hazel, this is Ned and Joe."

"Good to meet you," Hazel replied, as they each greeted her cordially, taking their hats from their heads for a moment. "You be sure to let me know what your favorite sweet things are and I'll rustle them up real soon."

The men smiled, glancing over at each other in delight. "Something like apple pie would be real good," said one, his blue eyes dancing. "I haven't had that in so long."

"And sweet biscuits," the other added, looking as though she were about to give him a wonderful gift. "That's awful kind of you, Mrs. Grant."

"Hazel," she corrected, as Stephen glanced over at her. "I'll have some ready for you in a couple of days' time, once I've settled in."

The two men thanked her at once, but Stephen soon interrupted their conversation and hurried them up, shooting a sharp glance at Hazel before digging his heels into the horse's sides and began to ride away.

Hazel coughed, waving away the cloud of dust with her apron as she watched them go. There such a sense of freedom that they carried with them, making her long to have that same independence. Stephen had made it clear he expected her to stay home all day and wait for him to take her to town later on in the week, but she needed things *now*. There was barely enough flour left to make another loaf of bread and certainly not enough for that *and* the apple pie she'd promised to make. She didn't even know where the apples were, or if Stephen had any.

Wandering back into the house and leaving the door wide open so that sunlight could stream through, Hazel looked around the room with a sharp eye. The first thing she'd need to do was make sure she had all she needed for dinner and breakfast for tomorrow. Then, she'd make a list of everything she needed to buy from town, as well as finish her unpacking. That would probably take her most of the morning, and she still had cleaning, cooking, and laundry to do.

Biting her lip, Hazel began to clear up the breakfast dishes, wondering how she was going to fit everything in. The last thing she wanted was for Stephen to come back to the house and find that his dinner wasn't ready and that his laundry hadn't been done. She needed to prove to him that she was a capable wife.

"Then I'll just head off to town tomorrow," she murmured to herself, as she found a rag to wipe the crumbs off the table. She would try to talk to Stephen about it again in the hope that he'd be happy for her to go there and back herself. After all, she knew how to hitch a horse to a wagon *and* how to drive it, so there was no good reason she couldn't.

But, then again, Stephen seemed to be a rather closed kind of man. A man who had strict ideas and expected them to be followed, a man who did things in order without really considering the feelings of others.

11

The following morning found Hazel in the stable, patiently hitching up the wagon to a rather grumpy-looking horse. It was the same one that had collected her from the station, so she was quite sure she had picked the right horse for the job.

Grimacing, she fiddled with one of the buckles, wishing she'd not managed to twist it. Her mind had been elsewhere, struggling with what had been said over dinner last night and then again at breakfast in the morning.

Finally managing to get the strap sorted out, she finished checking over the rest of the harness before climbing into the driving seat, picking up the reins and clicking to the horse. Thankfully, it began to move at once, quite used to pulling the wagon. Hazel smiled to herself as the sun hit her face as they came out of the barn. She was going to prove to Stephen that she didn't need his help when it came to running errands.

∼

As THE HORSE made its way to town—for Hazel didn't even need to direct it since it was quite clear it knew where it was going—she tried her best not to worry about what Stephen would say when he came home that evening. He might be rather angry with her, she supposed, but she was not about to stay home alone without any company for hours at a time. Of course, there was always a great deal for her to do, but that also included the absolute necessity of having everything she needed. For example, there was no flour left, which meant she could not make any more bread. Stephen had brushed it off when she'd mentioned it, telling her that he'd send Ned or Joe to fetch some when they came back from the pastures, but that wasn't good enough for Hazel. She needed the flour today. So why did Stephen seem so opposed to the idea of her leaving the ranch and then coming back?

Rolling her eyes, Hazel tried to relax and forget about Stephen. It was as if he wanted to keep her confined, keep her safe, whereas she wanted the freedom to go where she pleased, when she wanted. There wasn't even a question over what she should do. Stephen's word wasn't law, as far as she was concerned. He was being foolish, and she wasn't about to obey foolishness.

The town soon came into view. Making her way to the mercantile's, Hazel hopped down from the wagon and hitched her horse to the rail. Hoping that Mary was inside, Hazel made her way into the store, before being enveloped in a strong hug.

"Hazel!" Mary exclaimed, letting her go. "I've been waiting and waiting for you to come to town!"

Hazel laughed, her eyes twinkling. "It's only been a few days, Mary."

"Days without knowing whether you'd married him or not," Mary declared, looking quite delighted. "But I hear you've gone and married him, bless you, so now you're out there on that ol' ranch." She watched Hazel carefully for a moment, as though there was something she wanted to see in Hazel's expression. "Tell me, how do you like it out there?"

"I like it just fine," Hazel replied, with a slight shrug. "I mean, everything's very orderly, and it certainly don't feel like home yet, but I'm sure it will one day soon.

Mary nodded slowly, glancing all about her before speaking in hushed tones. "And how you getting on with that husband of yours?"

Hazel paused, thinking for a moment. "He's nice enough. We ain't got to know each other all that well yet, I suppose, but he don't seem a bad sort. Just likes things very organized, although I don't plan on being the kind of thing he *can* organize, no matter how hard he tries."

A slight frown appeared on Mary's face. "What do you mean?"

Glad that the shop was empty apart from one other customer, Hazel gave a slight shrug. "He wants me to stay back at the ranch, telling me that he'll take me to town to get what I need." She shook her head, letting out a long sigh. "I mean, he wants to take me to town, like I can't go by myself? I can do that just fine."

Concern flickered in Mary's eyes. "I know you can, but that doesn't mean you should," she replied slowly. "That man is just trying to keep you safe."

Hazel tossed her head. "I need things from town, and he won't let me come get them on my own. I don't understand his reasons, so I thought I'd show him that everything's just fine by coming on out here on my own anyway."

Mary looked as though she was going to say something more, only for her to clamp her mouth shut and shake her head, gesturing to all the things in the shop. "Just go on and take a look, Hazel. We've got almost everything you need. I'm sure of it."

"Does my husband have a tab here?" Hazel asked, immediately finding the flour she needed. "Can I add these things to it?"

Mary nodded, walking back behind the counter. "Sure, that's no problem. And my husband will help put all your purchases on the wagon."

Hazel smiled, feeling a little more at peace. Mary hadn't exactly agreed with her on every point, but at least she wasn't throwing her out of her shop and telling Hazel to go back to her husband's ranch until he was ready to take her. Pulling out the list from her pocket, Hazel began to look for all the things she needed, setting them out one at a time over at the desk.

"You sure Stephen's going to be all right with all this?" Mary asked, as she went to find the flour Hazel needed. "He's not a man who likes things done in a different way to what he's planned."

Hazel shrugged. "He's going to have to be. I ain't going to be a wife that's under her husband's thumb. The sooner he realizes that, the better things are going to be."

Mary's smile quirked. "Well, if you're sure. By the way, I was going to invite you to our quilting circle. The first one was last evening, but we'll be meeting again next week."

Appreciating Mary's invitation, Hazel smiled warmly. "I'd love to. Where is it held?"

"We just have it here, in the back," Mary replied, gesturing to a door that led through to her living quarters. "Frank, my husband, he goes off to the saloon for a while. In fact, most of the men folk do, unless they got little ones to look after. It'd sure to be nice to have another new face with us!"

"Then I'd be delighted to come along, although I'm not sure my sewing skills are going to be good enough." She bit her lip, a little concerned. "I'm good at darning and the like, but not so much quilting."

Mary laughed, beckoning her husband over. He was a tall, wiry man with a friendly face. After greeting her, he began to take her things out to the wagon, leaving Hazel free to talk.

"Now, don't you go fretting about things like that," Mary said and laughed, as she added up Hazel's purchases. "We'll teach you in whatever you're lacking. We're all at different stages. You ought to meet Betty! She is almost eighty years of age, and she is still quilting!"

As Hazel began to make her way home, she found that she was looking forward to getting to know a few more people in the town. It felt good to be able to start over, to be able to forget all that had gone before. Yes, she might still be a little jumpy when it was dark or when she was in that place all by herself, but she was finding it easier to put all thoughts of Christopher behind her. It was as though she'd been given a new lease of life, able to simply start over.

The ride back to the house was a nice one, given that it was a beautiful day with a good breeze. Hazel tipped her face up to the sun and took in a good long breath, a smile on her face. Once Stephen got home, he'd be able to see that she could manage things just fine on her own and that there was no need for his fretting. In fact, Hazel was quite sure he'd be really thankful that he wouldn't have to take her out to town and back, once he came round to the idea.

It took quite some time for her to unload all the packages from the wagon into the house and then, after that, to put the wagon away and rub down the horse, but by the time she was back in the house, she felt rather pleased with herself. She'd managed to accomplish all of that entirely on her own, and without any help from Stephen. It just went to show that she didn't need him to help her do all that stuff. She could manage just fine without him.

Glad that she finally had enough flour, Hazel set about making the apple pie she'd promised Ned and Joe, making sure there was one for her and Stephen as well. Humming to herself, she smiled happily as she began to prepare dinner, quite sure that everything would be just fine once Stephen saw all she'd accomplished.

"Did you go to town today?"

Ignoring the slight pink in Stephen's cheeks, Hazel smiled over at Ned and Joe and handed them the apple pie she had made. "It's still warm. I hope you enjoy it."

Ned and Joe wavered between grinning delightedly and looking over at Stephen, who was still glowering at her.

"Thank you very much, we'll be sure to enjoy this with our dinner," Ned replied, still glancing at Stephen. "Are we done for the day, Stephen?"

He didn't say a word, simply gestured for them to leave, and they took to their heels at once.

"Are you planning to wash up before we eat?" Hazel asked, trying to sound casual. "Dinner's on the table."

"You didn't answer my question," Stephen replied firmly. "Tell me, Hazel, did you go to town today?"

She shrugged, stepping in through the porch door. "And here I thought you'd be glad. It saves you having to take me."

He slammed the door tight behind him, making her jump. Closing her eyes for a moment, Hazel put one hand on her stomach and took a deep breath. He wasn't as happy as she'd thought he'd be. Instead, he was clearly very angry, and she grew afraid of the storm that was coming. Was this what Mary had meant when she'd said he wasn't exactly pleasant? Surely he'd never lay a finger on her? He hadn't seemed anything like Christopher so far.

But then you never saw that coming, she thought.

Swallowing hard, she turned around and tried to smile, her throat working furiously. "Stephen, I can do things like this myself. Can't you see that? I hitched up the horse and—"

"I said that I'd take you," he interrupted, stalking towards her with one finger pointed directly at her. "You're meant to bide by my rules."

Backing away just a little, Hazel lifted her chin and hid her fright as best she could. "I'm not going to be told what freedoms I can and can't have, Stephen. I'm not some poor little mite you need to care for."

He glared at her, his face red with anger. "It's the principle of the thing, Hazel. I'm your husband, and that means you obey."

"I won't obey ridiculous rules like forbidding me to go to town until you're around," she retorted, pushing away the ball of anxiety growing in her stomach. "I'm not about to be caged, Stephen."

That seemed to stop him in his tracks, his finger still pointed directly at her. His jaw was clenched, his eyes narrowed and still he said nothing.

"You're not going to tell me what I can and can't do," Hazel finished, her back now pressed against the wall. "I won't live that way. I can't."

His lip curled. "You're not the kind of wife I wanted, Hazel," he spat, his eyes fixed on hers. "I expected a biddable, quiet wife, not some free-spirited, unruly *child!*"

Hazel swallowed the lump in her throat, desperate to prove that his harsh words weren't hurting her. "I guess we don't always get what we want, do we?"

He stepped forward, and she reacted at once, wincing and

turning away from him. Her eyes closed tight, her hands reaching up to cover her face—but nothing came.

"What are you doing?"

Stephen's voice was quiet now, every single trace of anger gone entirely. When she opened one eye, she saw that he was staring at her in horror, his eyes wide.

"Did you think I was going to hit you, Hazel?"

She dropped her hands, fighting the inexplicable urge to burst into tears. "I don't know you very well yet, Stephen. I didn't know what you'd do."

His hand reached for hers, his fingers pressing hers gently. "I might have a temper, but I'd never lay a hand on you," he promised, a look of grief in his expression that she thought so little of him. "I'm not that kind of man."

Hazel looked down at their joined hands, something like relief spiraling all through her. "I'm glad to hear that," she whispered, not quite sure what else to say. "I-I guess we'd better eat dinner now."

Stephen held onto her hand for a moment longer before dropping it with a sigh. "I guess this means you're still going to head to town whenever you need something, don't it?"

She nodded, moving away from him as quickly as she could. "I've told you I won't be caged," she answered, trying to calm the quaking of her heart. "I meant it, Stephen. I'm sorry if I'm not the kind of woman you think you need, but I won't be anyone but myself. I can't let you change me. I won't."

She saw him sigh heavily, passing a hand over his eyes, before he came to sit across from her at the kitchen table. The meal was eaten in silence, with neither of them finding anything to say. Then, once the dishes were done, the table cleared, and the floor swept, he said goodnight and made his way to bed.

It was only once he'd closed the door behind him that Hazel felt safe enough to let her emotions come to the surface.

Leaning back in her rocking chair, she couldn't help but let the tears fall, although whether it was from fear or from relief, she couldn't quite say.

Who would have thought that going to town on her own would have caused so much strife?

12

Two weeks into his marriage and Stephen was still not sure about the woman he'd married. He certainly wasn't happy about her heading off into town on her own, given that he'd wanted to be the one to accompany her there. However, she was determined to get her own way, and he couldn't do anything to stop her, other than stay home all day to prevent her from leaving. Even then, he didn't think she'd listen to him.

This wasn't what he'd wanted; it wasn't what he'd hoped for. He'd expected a quiet, sweet-natured wife, who did as he asked and nothing more. His house would be kept neat and tidy, just as he liked it, and food would be on the table, morning, noon, and night.

Instead, he'd come home to find Hazel had rearranged some of his things or had made some alterations to something or other. In fact, one day he'd come home to discover that she'd removed the drapes in the lower part of the house and had replaced them entirely with a much brighter fabric in a pattern he didn't much like.

He'd told her as much, but she'd just tossed her head and told him he'd get used it. When he argued that he ought to have a say in things, she'd reminded him that he wasn't the one at home all day, as though her choice trumped his in some way.

It was infuriating.

And yet, there was something about her that he was growing to appreciate. He wasn't quite sure what it was, but it made living with her a little more bearable. Maybe it was the way she hummed to herself when she cleaned up after dinner, or the way her hair tumbled down her back when she was busy making breakfast. Whatever it was, it certainly soothed his angst. And on top of that, she'd managed to make more progress with his shy mare than he'd done in months. That said something about her, didn't it?

They were such different creatures, the two of them. He was orderly and focused, determined to have things his way and in a set fashion. Hazel liked to do things on the spur of the moment, suddenly deciding to ride into town after dinner just so she could see Mary. The first time she'd ridden to town when it was growing dark, he'd tried to stop her—to the point of walking all the way to the barn with her and making his voice heard. In the end, she'd looked back at him with fear in her eyes, shrinking away from him in the way she'd done before. His drive to win the disagreement died. He'd gone back to the house, his heart in his boots as he heard the horse ride away into the distance.

He hated that she had been so afraid of him. He couldn't understand why either, for he'd never once given her any suggestion that he'd be physical with her. There was no chance of him ever hurting his wife. He wasn't that kind of man, so what was it about him that made her think he was?

Shaking his head, Stephen rode up to the house alone, wondering whether or not to speak to her about it. Would she ever tell him about her past? He didn't even know why she'd offered to be his mail order bride, why she'd wanted to move away from her family. He knew, at least, that she had the rest of her family back home, he'd seen her write to them already. However, it did strike him as a little strange that she'd been so willing just to forget them all and head out to his ranch. It didn't seem as though there was some kind of strain between them, since she'd written such a long letter to them all—unless there was something he didn't know.

Taking his horse into the stables, Stephen quickly rubbed him down and let him out to the corral before heading indoors. He was looking forward to eating, which, he had to admit, was one good thing about Hazel; she really was an excellent cook.

The house was quiet when he stepped inside. From the appetizing aromas coming from the stove, he guessed that something was going to be ready real soon, but there was no sign of Hazel. A memory came flooding back to his mind, the scene in front of him reminding him of what had happened to him once before.

Frowning, he stuck his hat back on his head and strode out of the house, blinking in the sunshine. "Hazel?" he called, looking all about him. "Hazel? Where are you?"

A coil of worry formed in his stomach. Ned and Joe had been back for an hour or so already, but he didn't think she'd have gone to see them, not unless she was delivering another pie. Moving around to the back of the house, he tipped his hat back and scanned the horizon, only to see something moving down by the creek.

He broke into a run, suddenly terrified that she was struggling in the water, but soon came to a stop, arrested by the sight. Hazel was sitting on an old, overturned log that stretched out across the creek. Her feet were bare, and her skirts were pulled up high on her legs, showing her calves and ankles. She was humming to herself, bending forward to trail one finger in the flowing water. Something was so beautiful about the sight, it made something break open inside him, something that hadn't been a part of him for a real long time.

Stephen felt heat creep up his neck as he watched her, feeling as though he was intruding on something incredibly private—even though she was right out in the open.

Has she always been this lovely?

The thought had him frozen to the spot, blood roaring in his ears. Where had that come from? He wasn't meant to be thinking about his wife in that kind of way, not when he'd vowed never to even think about a woman that way. He'd been made a fool of once before, had his heart torn apart and scattered to the wind. When he'd finally put it all back together again, he'd built a cage around it and thrown away the key. No one was getting in there, not even his wife.

"Stephen!"

Jerking, he saw Hazel standing in the water, her cheeks brushed with pink.

"Sorry, I was just coming to look for you," he stammered, suddenly feeling a little out of his depth. "I came back home a little early this afternoon."

She smiled and sat back down on the log, her face tipped towards the sunshine. "Do you want to come sit by me?"

He cleared his throat, not liking the idea in the least. "Isn't dinner going to be ready soon?"

"Not yet," she replied, with a quick smile in his direction. "I only put it in just before I came out here. I had to wash my apron." She gestured to dripping garment just across from him, hanging from a nearby tree branch. "Are you sure you don't want to sit with me for a while? We are husband and wife after all. I think it's expected that we spend a little time with each other."

The twinkle in her eye and the small smile tugging at her lips made him flush and look away. "I don't think so."

For a moment, he wondered if she was lonely. After all, most evenings they spent in silence, each sitting in their own chair either out on the porch or in front of the stove if it was a cooler night. She was usually sewing or reading, and he just sat there, struggling to know what to do or to say to his rather difficult wife. That was what he hated the most, the fact that he truly wanted to find something to say. He wanted to talk to her without giving too much of himself away. He'd spent years building up a wall around himself and his past, and it wasn't one he intended to let her scale any time soon, if ever. Some things were meant to stay buried in the past.

"Sorry, Hazel. I don't' fancy joining you." *Even if you do make a rather alluring picture.*

"Why not, Stephen?"

Getting frustrated with her persistence, he stuck his hands in his pockets and shot her a dark look. "Because that would mean getting wet."

"And why is that so troublesome?"

Stephen opened his mouth to retort, but nothing came. He had nothing to say. Getting over to where she sat would mean walking directly into the creek, and he didn't particularly want to get wet.

"If you're going to worry about your boots getting wet, you know full well you can take them off," she continued, almost lazily. "I'm still waiting to hear a good excuse."

"I just don't want to get wet." His excuse sounded ridiculous, even to him, and yet he couldn't think of anything else to say. Here was his wife, offering him a chance to come sit by her and try and build on a relationship that was still fresh and new to them both, and he was turning her down just because he didn't want to get wet.

A look of disappointment came over her expression for just a moment, before she shrugged and looked away, wiping the displeasure from her face. "I'll be in real soon," she said, no longer even glancing at him. "I just want a few more minutes out here. The water's real nice."

Stephen couldn't move, his legs fixed to the ground. Why was he being so straight laced? Why couldn't he just do as she suggested, take off his boots and walk over to her?

Bowing his head for a moment, he let out a long, frustrated breath. He liked things in order and Hazel disrupted that part of his life. She was the kind of person to go wading in the creek just because she felt like it, whereas he struggled with the idea that dinner wasn't already on the table, same as it always was when he came home.

"Stephen?" Her voice was softer, practically forcing him to look up at her. "Is something wrong?" Her eyes were worried, a slight frown on her face. Was she worried he was about to reprimand her for something again? He couldn't blame her for that, considering that was almost all he ever did.

"No, nothing's wrong," he muttered, finally managing to turn away from her. "I'll see you inside."

As he walked away, something began to unfurl itself inside him. It was as though he *wanted* to go and do as she'd asked and sit by her. He liked routine and order, and she knew that full well, and still, she was trying to get him to do something out of the ordinary, something that he hadn't ever thought to do before. He'd never thought about taking off his boots and wade in the creek, but the fact that Hazel had done it and had invited him to join her, meant that something in him wanted to do just that.

And yet, he couldn't bring himself to do it.

"She's having an effect on me."

Throwing his hat down on the table, Stephen went off into

his room to change, growing frustrated with himself. Why was she getting him all worked up like this? It had been a simple thing she'd asked him, and he had every right to say no. So, why was he questioning what he'd done? Why was he going over and over it in his mind, frustrated with his own indecision? It just didn't make sense.

Changing quickly, Stephen paused as he heard Hazel come on back into the house, the sound of her humming reaching his ears. She brightened the whole house by her presence, his heart jumping in his chest as he heard her break into song.

Groaning, he sat down on the bed and put his head in his hands, running them through his hair. This couldn't be happening. He couldn't let it happen. What he couldn't do was fall in love with his wife, especially after what had happened the last time he'd done that. It wasn't worth the pain. Love meant allowing yourself to be vulnerable and open, giving up your own way for the sake of the one you loved.

Stephen didn't want that. He needed Hazel to keep her distance in the same way he kept his. A marriage that was built on reliance and responsibility, yes, but not on love. That wasn't the kind of life he wanted.

ONCE DINNER WAS OVER, Stephen sat down in his chair by the fire and began to rock, listening to Hazel humming gently as she fixed the coffee. She knew just how he liked it and brought it over to him, her fingers brushing his as she handed it to him. Stephen felt his gut clench, as though aware of just how close she was to him, but he ignored it completely. After thanking her quickly, he lapsed into silence.

Hazel sat down next to him, rocking gently in her chair as she got on with some darning, apparently quite content with the silence between them. Stephen swallowed his coffee, thinking it tasted a little bitterer than usual. He didn't like what was going on in his heart, didn't like that she was making him question why he did things.

"I'm going to go to the quilting circle tomorrow night," Hazel said quietly. "Some of the other husbands get together for a drink while their wives do their sewing." She glanced at him, a smile on her face. "I wondered if you wanted to go."

There she was again, trying to push him into doing something different. "No, I don't want to go."

"You sure?" she asked, rocking gently back and forth. "I never see you talking to anyone at church on Sundays, and out here, it's only just me—as well as Ned and Joe, I suppose, but they ain't really your friends."

"Neither are you."

The words left his mouth before he could stop them, shooting out from him like a bullet from a gun.

The light in Hazel's eyes began to dim, and she looked away from him, not saying a single word. Stephen closed his eyes and bit down on his tongue, tasting blood. He hadn't meant that, not really. He had just been upset with what she'd said, struggling against the way she was pushing at him to change his way of life. He was quite happy here. There was no reason for him to go to town, to drink with the other husbands. Friends weren't necessary. Life had taught him that even the closest friend could do the most terrible of things.

" Hazel, I—"

She cleared her throat, getting up from her chair and turning her back to him. Her back was straight, her head held high, and yet she didn't turn to look at him. "I think I'll go to bed now," she said, her voice thick with whatever emotion she was trying to hide from him. "I'm feeling rather tired. Goodnight, Stephen. I hope you sleep well."

He didn't know what to say, his mind scrambling to find a way to apologize to her, to tell her that he hadn't meant any of that, but it all came too late. The door was already closed behind her, the stairs creaking as she made her way up the stairs, leaving him alone with his tormented thoughts.

13

Over the next two weeks, Hazel found herself falling into some kind of a routine. She'd head into town twice a week, once for her goods and once for the quilting circle. On Sundays, of course, they'd head into town together for church, although they spent the rest of the day entirely apart from each other. He'd go off into the barn to do something, whereas she'd either read or go out for a ride on her own. She was quite used to riding alone now and had begun to get to know the land around her pretty well. The only thing she didn't have was her own horse.

Not that it mattered, life was pretty good regardless. She had a house that was slowly becoming a home, a freedom that she had battled to keep, and a mind that was forgetting all about Christopher. Now that she knew for certain that Stephen wasn't going to hurt her in any way, she began to trust him.

She still didn't like it when he came too close, her stomach tightening with a strange mixture of worry and expectation, but that was slowly getting better. He clearly didn't want any kind of affection from her, and she was happy not to give it. The words he'd spoken to her so harshly still gnawed at her mind, still dogged her thoughts. He'd muttered an apology the following morning, which she'd accepted, but she'd not stopped wondering why he'd said it in the first place. Was it to deliberately hurt her feelings? Or did he think she was getting too close, and now he was determined to push her away somehow?

One other thing still troubled her, too. He still seemed to be angry with her a lot of the time. In fact, practically all of the time. His jaw would jut out, his eyes darkening as he watched her, whether that was when she talked about the quilting circle or who she'd met in town that day. He'd come to find her paddling in the creek on more than one occasion, and every time, he refused her suggestion that he join her and stormed back into the house.

He never spoke to her about whatever it was that was troubling him, though something within her wanted to know. Was it just that he didn't like her refusal to do as he asked? Or was there something deeper going on?

Shaking her head to herself, Hazel leaned on the corral fence and murmured gently to the beautiful, shy mare whom she'd named Daisy. Apparently, Stephen had wanted very little to do with the creature, since he'd never been able to get much out of her, and so he'd allowed Hazel to give her a name. He'd rolled his eyes at her choice, but she'd ignored him, feeling a connection with the animal that she couldn't express. Remembering a day last week when she'd watched as Stephen rode the mare, becoming aware of just how hard he'd been pulling at her mouth. She ran a troubled eye over the horse's mouth and nose, hoping there was no injury there.

"You just need a gentle hand, don't you?" she whispered, laughing as the mare nickered and sniffed at her hand, evidently looking for some sugar.

"Don't you go spoiling her now."

It took everything in Hazel's power not to roll her eyes,

hating that Stephen could be so harsh with his horses. "I'll spoil her if I like, Stephen, since it's clear she doesn't respond to anger." She shot him a pointed look, trying not to notice just how handsome he looked against the pink and orange horizon.

His green eyes filled with irritation as he frowned, looking from her to the mare. "You really think my ways don't work?"

"I know they don't," Hazel replied truthfully. "Do you really think you can get a creature like this to do what you want if you're forceful enough?" She lifted her eyebrows, rather aware that she was speaking to him of more than just the horse. He seemed to notice it, too, since he looked away from her almost at once, turning himself to face the corral a little more.

"It's always worked before," he muttered, not looking at her. "I don't see why this one should be any different."

Hazel paused for a moment, considering what she was going to say. Stephen didn't like her blunt ways and responded rather badly to them. So, out of consideration for him, she was trying to think before she spoke, making sure not to appear overbearing.

"You haven't broken that many horses here, have you?" she asked, hoping her tone didn't sound condescending. "I think you said only two others?"

"Three before this one," he said, leaning his chin on his arms as they rested on the fence post. "They were all easy."

"Well, this one is afraid of you," Hazel said pointedly. "She's a gentle creature with a free spirit. She needs understanding, not someone trying to force her to bend to his will."

He snorted but didn't immediately contradict her. "You think you can do better?"

Not afraid of a challenge, Hazel lifted her chin and grinned at him. "Saddle her up, cowboy. I'll show you how it's done."

Color shot up his neck and into his face, his eyes fixed on hers as she laughed, as though her teasing tone had caught him entirely off guard. Hazel couldn't help but laugh as he stumbled away from her, one hand rubbing the back of his neck. Was it because he had been expecting her to refuse? He should know her better by now.

Something warm curled in her stomach as she watched him carry things out one at a time. He was strong and purposeful in his movements, hefting the saddle onto the mare's back with ease. The mare stood calmly as Hazel held the bridle, as though she knew it would be Hazel on her back today, not Stephen.

"Ready?"

She smiled and stepped forward, putting one foot into his hands. He helped her up and, with a quick push, she was settling into the saddle.

"Are you sure about this now, Hazel?" he asked, as she adjusted her seat. "I mean, I didn't have a lot of luck."

Ignoring his concerns, she looked down at him, already feeling quite at peace on Daisy's back. "How abouts we go for a ride?"

He frowned. "Now? It's late. I thought we'd be turning in soon."

"Yes, but tomorrow is Sunday," she reminded him, with a quick smile. "That means no going out to the pastures, no chores, no nothing."

"Except the service."

A little frustrated, Hazel bit back her sharp reply. "Yes, there is the service, but my point is that we don't need to worry so much about retiring. Don't you want to come riding with me?"

She held her breath, as he looked up at her, frowning a little. She'd been trying to reach out to him a little more, but so far he'd refused her at every turn. It was as if he couldn't quite bring himself to change, couldn't quite manage to do things her way. Whilst she knew he didn't want any kind of affection and certainly nothing like love between them, that didn't mean that they couldn't have a friendship, right? But friendship meant that they would have to spend time together—instead of simply living together in the same house but hardly saying a word to each other in the evenings. She wanted more than just the silence he was apparently so used to.

"I think I'd best turn in."

Her shoulders slumped, but she lifted her chin and tried to smile, pretending it didn't matter to her. "Well, I guess I'll see you later."

"You're not going out there on your own?"

She laughed and nudged Daisy into a trot, making her way to the gate of the corral which, thankfully, he'd left open when he'd gone to get the things from the stable. "Stephen, I've been out riding here plenty times. I'll be just fine."

"Hazel, I'm not happy about this."

She shrugged, looking back at him. "Then I guess you'd better get your own horse saddled."

Not waiting to hear another word from him, Hazel dug her heels in and set off in a gallop, keeping her head low as Daisy did exactly what Hazel asked. The mare responded beautifully to everything Hazel did, and it was a good few minutes before Hazel pulled the reins and brought her back to a walk.

"My goodness," she breathed, her heart beating rapidly in her chest. "Daisy, you are a dream to ride."

The sound of thundering hooves came from behind her, and twisting around in her seat, Hazel saw none other than her husband coming after her, his own horse in a full gallop. Daisy snorted nervously, but Hazel patted her neck with a calm hand, settling her back down.

A burst of warmth in her heart had her smiling broadly as Stephen reined his horse in, unable to stop herself from grinning at him.

"I see you came."

"I had no choice," he muttered, glowering at her. "I have a stubborn wife, who won't do what she's asked."

"You can't still be thinking I'm ever going to be the wife you hoped for," Hazel replied lightly, despite the slicing pain in her heart. "I thought you knew that wouldn't ever be the case."

Something lifted in his expression, removing the frown from his face. "I guess I have accepted it," he said, with a small smile that only just reached his eyes. "How did you find Daisy?"

Hazel stroked the horse's neck and sighed happily. "She's wonderful to ride. It's like she knows what I'm going to ask for before I actually do anything."

Stephen sighed and shook his head, a look of frustration on his face. "That's more than I ever got her to do."

"Gentleness and understanding," Hazel reminded him, nudging Daisy into a walk. "Not sheer brute strength. She doesn't understand that."

They rode for a short time in silence, but Hazel felt as though her heart was about to burst. This was the first time Stephen had ever agreed to do something she'd suggested, the first time he'd stepped away from his regimented routine and had followed her. She hadn't expected that to bring her so much joy, but the happiness in her heart could not be denied. The horizon lay before them, the reds and pinks and oranges lighting up the plains. Closing her eyes, Hazel smiled softly to herself, letting go of the reins and stretching her arms out wide. Finally, she felt as though she belonged.

"Careful!"

Stephen caught her hand, giving her a slight shove back towards the front of her horse.

"Pick up those reins."

Hazel laughed and shook her head. "Why? Daisy is just fine, and I trust her not to run off just because she pleases it."

He frowned, his lips in a thin line. "It would make me feel better if you picked them up."

Hazel was about to refuse, but then she saw the concern in his expression. He really was worried about her, and much to her surprise, she wanted to relieve that worry even if it meant doing something she didn't particularly want to do.

"I've got them," she murmured, picking them up as she held his gaze. "I'm quite safe, Stephen."

She watched, as he took a long breath, clearly a little relieved. She needed to remember just how much it had taken for him to come out here with her. Now wasn't the time to tease him and try to push him further.

"Do you mind if we head on back?" he asked, turning his horse around. "It'll be getting dark soon, and I would like to have the horses safe in the barn by then."

Hazel nodded, seeing the surprise on his face as she did as he asked without question. How much she wanted to explain to him that she wasn't just being difficult for the sake of it, that she needed the freedom to make her own decisions when he wasn't around. However, at times like these, she was happy to do as he asked. It seemed an almost impossible concept to explain, and as they rode back home, Hazel found that she just didn't have the words to even begin.

ONCE BACK AT THE RANCH, Hazel waited for Stephen to help her down from the horse, her mouth going dry as she realized she was going to have to lean down into his arms. All the other times she'd ridden alone, she'd used the mounting block in the stables, or even a bale of hay, to get on and off the horse. Out in the corral, she had no other choice but to lean into his arms.

He looked up at her, his gaze fixed. Something softened in

his expression as he saw her hesitate, an understanding that she was worried about something.

Hazel couldn't put it into words. How could she explain to him what had happened with Christopher? How could she tell him that, even though she'd forgotten Christopher, her heart still slammed violently into her chest whenever Stephen got too near?

"Come on, Hazel," he said quietly. "I'm not going to drop you."

She tried to laugh, a choking sound escaping from her throat. "I never even thought of that," she managed to say, her tongue like sandpaper as she leaned down, swinging one leg over the saddle.

The movement seemed to surprise Daisy, who jumped and danced a few steps, which meant that Hazel practically fell out of the saddle. Stephen caught her at once, holding her tightly as he lowered her to the ground.

Hazel couldn't breathe. She couldn't move. His hands were still on her waist, holding her there so gently, without any of the strength she'd seen earlier. She could step away if she wanted and he'd let her go; she *knew* he'd let her go.

So why wasn't she moving?

The last rays of sunlight hit his face, his features highlighted with gold. Hazel felt her breath catch as she stood there, simply taking him in. There was no frown on his face, no anger, no frustration. Those lines had disappeared, and in their place, was a questioning look, as though he didn't quite understand all that was going on. It was an expression she was sure she mirrored, her eyes widening as he began to lower his head.

They had fought like cat and dog. Now, here they were, standing in the middle of the corral, and he was about to kiss her. Hazel didn't move, didn't struggle, didn't run. Instead, she just closed her eyes and waited, trying to sort out all her conflicted feelings. Part of her screamed at her to run, remembering the last time she'd been kissed, whilst the other part told her to stay, to wait to see what he would do. Maybe this was a way for her to forget what Christopher had done, a way to replace those terrible memories with new ones.

He is not like Christopher, she repeated to herself over and over again. *Stephen is not like Christopher.*

The kiss never came. Instead, Hazel felt his hands drop from her waist and felt the loss of his presence as he stood back. As he cleared his throat, she opened her eyes and looked at him, feeling something like embarrassment crawl all through her. Had she misjudged things? Had she misjudged him?

"I think you'd better keep Daisy," he said gruffly, pulling off his hat and running one hand through his hair. "She isn't for me, that's for sure."

Hazel blinked, hardly able to believe what she'd heard. "You're giving me a horse?"

He shrugged and looked away, one boot scuffing in the dust. "Sure, I mean...if you want her."

Without knowing what she was doing, Hazel threw herself at him, her arms going around his neck. She could hardly believe that he was giving her something so precious, something that would be all her own.

"Thank you, Stephen," she breathed, tears pricking at the corner of her eyes. "Thank you. I'll take good care of her."

He cleared his throat again and gave her a slightly self-conscious smile as she stepped back. "I know you will, Hazel. I'm not saying I like you riding off into town on your own, but I guess that's been talked about once too often. At least you've got your own horse now, so you won't be using mine." His lips curved into a smile, his eyes twinkling at her. It was such a change in his expression, that for a moment, Hazel was robbed of speech, caught by the happiness she saw.

"I'll rub the horses down," he said, grasping Daisy's bridle and clicking to his own horse. "Why don't you head on in?"

Hazel nodded and smiled, the lump in her throat aching so much she could hardly speak. "I will. Thank you, Stephen."

He smiled back at her before turning around and heading towards the barn, leaving her to walk back to the house on her own.

Once inside, Hazel closed the door and leaned back against it, feeling as though she might burst from happiness. Finally, after all her attempts, Stephen had finally done something she'd asked of him. He'd come out on a ride with her when she knew he wanted to stick to his usual routine and head on in. It might not have been a lot, but it meant a great deal to Hazel. Now, he'd given her one of his horses to use as her very own! It was a kindness she hadn't expected from him. The gesture took her breath away, her heart swelling with gladness.

"There's more to him than I think even he knows," she said to herself, heading on up the stairs. She just had to hope that what they'd started would carry on even more. She wanted to have a husband who smiled and laughed and talked with her, not a silent, stony-faced man who had nothing to say. Whatever it was that had been troubling him about her and their marriage, Hazel had to hope that he'd be able to move past it now and onto better things. On to a better future for them both.

But, as she got changed into her night things, a rather uncomfortable truth hit Hazel full on. If she wanted them to grow in their relationship, if she wanted them to have a solid friendship, then that meant she was going to have to start being honest with him. There were so many things she hadn't told him about, not even much about her family or her childhood. She certainly hadn't told him about Christopher, especially since she hadn't wanted to even so much as think about him.

Would she have to be the one to take the first step, to be the one to open herself up and tell him about her past? How could they have a future together when he didn't really know her at all? All he knew was that he didn't like her way of living her life and didn't understand that freedom she so desperately craved. Would he understand her better if she told him more? Would she be able to understand his reasons behind his need to have everything so determined?

Her mind filled with thoughts and questions, Hazel made her way to bed, aware that Stephen was moving through the house downstairs. It was a long time before she closed her eyes and even longer until she finally fell asleep.

14

S tephen looked at himself in the mirror, making sure his hair was neatly combed. It had been a hard day out with the cattle, moving them a little further along the pastures, and he was tired. Having dragged himself into the house, he'd been ushered into the bedroom to clean up and change, and now here he was, running a comb through his hair.

He stopped, the comb dropping from his fingers. What was he doing? Why was he making such an effort for his wife? She didn't care if he came to the table with hair that stuck up all over the place; she only cared that he wasn't going to put dust and sand all over the table!

He reached to run his fingers through his hair, to prove that he didn't need to make an effort for Hazel, but he couldn't quite bring himself to do it.

Closing his eyes, Stephen drew in a long breath. This week had been so different from the first few weeks of their marriage. Hazel had become easier to live with for some reason. He wasn't as bothered by her riding into town, or her paddling in the creek on a hot day. She was willing to do what he asked sometimes, but other times pushed for what she wanted. That was just a part of her, he guessed, and so life had become a little easier.

Was it that she had changed, or had he just begun to accept the situation for what it was?

A frown crossed his brow as he considered things, his lips twisting. No, it had to be her. She'd been much more talkative of late, and he'd found that he wanted to listen. She'd told him all about her life back home, going into detail about how she'd felt about her parents moving to her brother-in-law's ranch. When she'd described her hometown, he'd caught himself listening intently, hanging on to every word. The more she talked, the more he felt he knew her. She was like a rose, slowly coming into bloom right before his eyes. He began to appreciate her company.

Instead of just looking forward to coming home for the food, Stephen began to look forward to coming home to his wife. Her ready smile brought a happiness to his heart he couldn't explain, her welcome always making him feel as though he were appreciated. Yes, something had changed, but he couldn't quite work out what it was.

He thought back to the night almost a week ago when she'd been in his arms, not moving, not speaking. She'd looked up at him with eyes that spoke of confusion and wonder, as though not quite certain about what he planned to do. The truth was, he hadn't been certain either, finding himself caught up with her entirely. He hadn't wanted to move away from her, too afraid that he'd shatter whatever it was that had wrapped itself around them.

He'd almost kissed her.

Dropping his head in his hands, Stephen groaned aloud, sitting down on the edge of his bed. He'd pushed that thought away from his mind for days now, and still it dogged him. He hadn't wanted to admit it, even to himself, but he knew that the truth was undeniable. When she'd looked up at him, he had felt his heart stir. Hazel had looked so stunningly beautiful that he'd hardly been able to breathe, his heart filling with emotion. And then, he'd moved away, knowing he couldn't do it.

He didn't want to fall in love with his wife and had been vehemently denying to himself that he felt anything for her. Still, his feelings grew. They were growing closer, which he certainly appreciated, but he'd never wanted anything more than friendship between them. There wasn't any expectation of more than that.

"Are you coming?"

Closing his eyes, Stephen ran one hand down his face before getting up, setting his shoulders. "Yes." He would have to just push those thoughts away again, just like he'd been doing every day since last Saturday evening.

"I thought you deserved a good meal this evening, so I've made you everything I knew you'd enjoy," Hazel said and smiled as he came in. Stephen stopped short, staring at the table that was filled with everything he could ever dream of. He closed his eyes tightly and then opened them again, hardly able to believe that she'd done this.

"Why?" he asked softly, moving forward to sit across from her. "Why did you do this?"

She shrugged, her cheeks pink as she smiled at him. "I wanted you to know how much I appreciate how well you take care of...this place. And me."

"Oh." Stephen didn't know what to say, the words dying on his lips.

Bowing her head, Hazel waited for him to say the blessing. Still taken aback by what she'd done, Stephen murmured a prayer. When he opened his eyes, he saw her holding out the basket of freshly made rolls to him.

"Help yourself," she said, with a quick smile. "There should be more than enough for us to have some again tomorrow and even Sunday!" Taking a roll for herself, she tucked in a stray tendril of hair and began to butter it.

Stephen couldn't take his eyes off her.

This wasn't the woman he had first met, so hard and brash. She was softer now, kind and compassionate. It was as though, in allowing her the freedom she demanded, he'd allowed the rest of her character to shine through. Had she been right about how he'd treated Daisy? After all, the mare had responded to her tenderness and understanding instead of his firm hand and demanding nature. Was the way he had treated Hazel exactly the same? When he'd been hard and unyielding, she'd refused to even consider what he was saying, determined to struggle against him. And now, when he had simply allowed her the freedom she wanted, when he listened to her conversation, she'd responded with tenderness and compassion.

"You're not eating."

Hazel's soft voice broke into his thoughts, making him start in surprise. "Sorry."

"You're not disappointed, are you? Did I miss something?"

There it was again, the tiniest hint of her vulnerability. It wasn't often she showed it, but now that she had, all he wanted to do was reassure her.

"I'm overwhelmed by it," he said at once, reaching across the table to take her hand. She grasped it readily, without jerking away as he thought she might. "You've taken my breath away, Hazel."

She blushed and looked away, a smile on her face. "I'm glad, Stephen. I want this to be a happy home."

"So do I," he agreed, looking over at her and letting go of her hand. "I think we've reached a better place."

Her smile wobbled. "Yes, I'd agree, but there's something important that I need to share with you."

A frown immediately crossed his face. "Oh?"

She shook her head and shrugged. "It can wait. Let's eat first."

BY THE TIME the meal was over, Stephen had almost forgotten that Hazel had something she wanted to share with him. They'd talked about so many other things, and he'd enjoyed every minute of their conversation.

"Do you mind if I tell you now what I wanted to say?"

Stephen took the coffee cup from her as he sat in his rocking chair, seeing the strain on her face. "Of course. I'm sorry I forgot. I should have asked you sooner."

"No, don't worry," came the reply. "I know I got rather distracted, too." Taking in a deep breath, she began to walk up and down in front of the stove, her fingers twining together as she walked. Clearly, this was something that had troubled her deeply.

"I was in love before. I mean, I *thought* I was in love. With a young man named Christopher."

Stephen frowned, watching her walk up and down the room. That wasn't what he had expected to hear. "Oh?"

"He was from my town, and we had something of a friendship for a while, but it was a friendship that developed into something more."

A stone dropped into Stephen's stomach. Was she about to tell him that she was ruined and that the only reason she'd married him was so that she didn't have to leave her town in disgrace? Had she brought shame to her family? Did they no longer want her in their home?

"I believed that Christopher loved me," she continued, a little unsteadily. "I mean, he never really committed to me, and we never really spoke about the future, but in my mind, I thought we were to be married." She glanced at him, her cheeks pale. "It turned out that marriage wasn't what was on his mind."

The coffee cup fell from his hands, clattering to the floor.

"No," he breathed, staring at her as though she were, somehow, telling him untruths. "You cannot mean that he—?"

"He tried, but he didn't succeed," she said quickly, the words tumbling from her mouth. "I managed to get home safely, but I couldn't go out there again. The whole town soon knew about it. My father had to be restrained once he discovered what had happened."

Just as any father would react, Stephen thought, a white hot anger coursing through his veins.

"The reason I married you is so that I could get away," she said quietly. "I couldn't be in that town any longer, not when he was still there and not when the places I'd once loved had become spoiled."

Understanding blossomed. "That's why you've jerked away from me so often," he said slowly. "You're afraid I'm just like him."

She shook her head fervently and came towards him, an uncertain look on her face. "No, Stephen, not any more. I mean, I did initially think that you were, but then as I got to know you, I realized that you couldn't be like him. There's none of that in you."

His throat constricted at the vulnerability on her face, the anxiety written in her eyes. She was waiting for him to confirm that he believed her, that he didn't hold it against her.

"Thank you for trusting me enough to tell me," he said softly, reaching for her hand and feeling just how cold it was. "I can understand you better now that I know."

"That's what I want," she replied, her lips trembling just a little, her eyes glassy. "It's been so difficult not being able to explain, but I hope you understand now. I couldn't give in to your demands; I couldn't have you take away my freedom from me. Not after what happened."

He got to his feet and held her tight against him, feeling her begin to shake. His anger burned against the man who had hurt her, wishing that he lived nearby so that he could do something more about it. His heart ached for Hazel, for all she had been through, for all she had suffered. He understood what it was like to believe you were loved in return, only for that all to be taken away.

Should I tell her my own story?

His mind closed at once, refusing to allow him to even consider doing such a thing. That was his own pain, his own grief. It was his to deal with, his to dwell on as he chose. He didn't need to be as open with Hazel.

Her tears dampened his shirt as she clung to him, more exposed than he had ever seen her before. Grateful that she had been willing to tell him such a difficult story, he continued to hold her tightly, aware of her arms creeping around his neck. He allowed them to remain there, his eyes slowly closing as he rested his cheek against the top of her head.

Eventually, her sobs began to lessen until she became quiet in his arms. He didn't know how long he'd held her for, time beginning to slow around them. This felt right, *more* than right; it was as though she belonged.

The usual noises began to rebel against what he was feeling, but he quieted them instead of allowing them to speak. He couldn't explain what was going on, but the peace that filled him wasn't something he was willing to throw away. He held her for a long time, until finally she lifted her head.

Her eyes looked into his, clearer than he had ever seen them before. Her cheeks were still damp, and he ran his thumb down one of them gently, wiping it away. Nothing was said between them, not even when his hand moved to her hair and began to tug the pins out of them one by one.

It was as though he were in a dream, as though he were not the one actually doing this. Her hair was soft, framing her face as it fell down over her shoulders and back. He ran his fingers through it, never taking his eyes away from hers.

When she lifted her face to his, Stephen didn't hesitate. His lips touched hers gently, her hands tightening around his neck. A sweetness was in her kiss he hadn't expected, a burst of happiness sending shivers all through him. Angling his head, he deepened the kiss and pulled her tight against him, promising with his kiss that he would never let her go. She would never have to face that kind of danger again. Her honesty and openness would not be discarded, not after what she had shared. For the first time in years, Stephen felt at peace.

All until he woke the following morning and realized what he had done.

15

Hazel woke the next day with a smile on her face and a love in her heart that had taken root the night before. Sharing her heart with Stephen had been both terrifying and rewarding, the pain sweeping through her all over again. Reliving the nightmare had been hard, but now, in seeing the response from Stephen, she knew it had been worth it.

When he'd taken her in his arms, she'd gone willingly, knowing that she could relax into his strength. More than just a comfort had been there. He had held her as though he would never let her go, his tender strength bringing her the relief she needed.

His kiss had been unexpected, but welcome. Finally, Hazel realized that she cared more for this man than just a friendly affection. Whatever had grown between them had blossomed into more than just a familiarity, and a deep-rooted connection had formed. The beginnings of love. She could not wait to see what their future held now.

A vision of children, of a happy family around the kitchen

table, sprang into her mind, making her want to cry out with joy. She had forgotten those dreams the moment Christopher had pressed himself onto her, but now, despite all their difficulties, Stephen had brought those back to her.

She could barely take it in.

They'd parted last evening with barely anything more said between them. He'd been nothing but respectful. There had been no cajoling, no urging for her to come to his bed. It was as if he had been just as surprised by their kiss as she had been. The light in his eyes had given hope that things could only continue to grow between them.

Getting out of bed, Hazel took her time to dress, carefully pinning up her hair in a somewhat different style than usual. She flushed as she realized what she was doing, smiling to herself as she made her way down the stairs.

Stephen was nowhere to be seen.

Frowning, she saw a note on the table, one hastily written. Going to pick it up, she flipped it open and saw Stephen's scrawl penning only two short lines.

'I'm sorry, Hazel. I can't do this. Please go to town and stay with Mary until I can make arrangements.

Stephen.'

Hazel read it over two or three times, her hands beginning to tremble. Her legs grew weak, her heart almost coming to a complete stop such was the shock of it. This couldn't really be Stephen's writing, could it?

She read it over again, her mind going blank. She had no idea what he meant by "I can't do this." He wanted her to go and stay with Mary until he could make arrangements? Arrangements for what? Divorce? Did he plan on sending her back home without explanation?

The letter fluttered to the floor as she sat forward, putting her elbows on her knees and burying her head in her hands.

She waited for the tears to come but none did. Her eyes remained dry, something like anger beginning to burn in her heart.

Was this because of what she'd revealed to him last night? Was this to do with her past, to do with Christopher?

Shaking her head, Hazel got to her feet and began to walk up and down, much as she had done last evening. No, that could not be the case. He had listened to her and had tried to comfort her as best he could, before kissing her gently. He would not have done that if he hadn't truly felt something for her!

Picking up the letter, Hazel read it over again before tearing it up into small pieces, letting them flutter to the floor. Did he really think that she'd just do as he asked, that she'd just go and stay with Mary before being sent home? Hadn't he learned anything about her?

Stamping her foot, Hazel marched to the front door and flung the door open, expecting to see him standing there. Instead, all she could see were the horses, each lifting their heads as they spotted her. Stephen was nowhere to be seen.

Stopping for a moment, Hazel closed her eyes and took in a few deep breaths, trying her best to think clearly despite the turmoil that was going on in her heart. Stephen was clearly upset about something, although she didn't know what. Where would he have gone? To town? To the pastures? She wasn't expecting him to work today, but that didn't mean he wouldn't have ridden out to the cattle in the hope of getting away from her. So what could she do? Chewing on her lip, Hazel opened her eyes and leaned on the porch rail, trying to think clearly.

Her first choice was to do just as he'd asked and go to Mary's home and wait for him to come to her with an explanation. Then, she'd be told what would be happening next. Hazel snorted, shaking her head to herself. That wasn't an option she would be taking, and she was surprised that Stephen even thought she would do that.

The second choice she had was to stay here and wait. He'd have to come back to the ranch sometime, and they could talk then—if he'd even talk to her. Maybe he'd retreat into himself, the silent man sitting in the rocking chair she'd once known.

Then, the only other thing she could do was go and look for him. She frowned, knowing that she had no knowledge of the pastures and that to go out there now would be foolish. Could she go to town? Could she speak to Mary and find out what she knew?

That idea gave her a sense of purpose, no longer feeling as lost and as confused as she did when she first read the letter. Mary had made a few comments about Stephen before, but had never said anything directly.

"Then maybe it's time I find out the truth about my husband," Hazel said to herself, her voice loud and filled with determination. "If he won't tell me what's making him do this, then I'll find out for myself."

Hurrying towards the barn, she quickly found Daisy and saddled her up quickly, her heart beginning to pound as she did so. She still couldn't believe that Stephen had written that letter, that he had been so callous as to push her away right after they had been closer than they'd ever been before.

She paused, her hands stilling on the reins. Was this why he had written that note? Was their kiss too much for him? A sudden memory of the day they had married caught her, forcing her to remember how he'd stood away from her, an uncertain look in his eyes. Had he married before? Had he loved before? Was this hardness, this fear of giving her the freedom she wanted, all stemmed from something like that?

"I won't know until I ask Mary," she said aloud, pressing her heels into Daisy's sides and making her way to town.

THE TOWN WAS quiet when she got there, most likely because it was early morning still and not everyone was up and about. Much to her frustration, the mercantile was still closed, which only went to show just how early she was.

Not sure what to do, Hazel tied Daisy to the rail and began to wander around town, greeting a few familiar faces. One thing was for sure, Stephen was not there. Not yet, anyway. Whatever arrangements he was making, they weren't here.

"Hazel? Is that you?"

Spinning around, Hazel saw Mary step out of the mercantile, tying her apron around her waist.

"Oh, Mary," she whispered, hurrying towards her. Mary enveloped her in a hug almost at once, evidently seeing the pain on Hazel's face.

"Whatever's happened?" she asked, as Hazel felt herself crumple. "This isn't the Hazel I know."

Hazel wanted to be that strong woman she'd always been, but in the face of Mary's compassion, her heart had torn to pieces and she'd felt herself break.

"I don't know where Stephen is," she whispered, tears pooling in her eyes. "He left me a note."

Mary stepped back and took Hazel's hands in her own, a serious expression on her face. "Come on in. We need to talk. Not out here where everyone can see you."

Glancing around her and relieved to see that there was no one else there, Hazel followed Mary inside, not even raising a smile when she shooed Frank away to make tea.

"Now, you sit down there and tell me everything," Mary said, leading her into the kitchen at the back of the shop. "From the look on your face, I'd say you've had something of a shock."

Haltingly, Hazel began to explain all that had happened, aware of the slow-growing horror written on Mary's face.

"I don't understand why he's doing this," she finished, hardly able to keep her tears back. "I thought to come here and speak to you—to speak to someone who knows my husband better than I do. I can' t go back home, not now. Not when..." her voice trailed off, her eyes drifting away from Mary's gaze.

"Not when you love him," Mary said quietly. "Hazel, I'd be wrong to pretend I ain't been hoping for this for a while now, but I never thought that boy would do anything so stupid as to run away from his feelings!"

"What happened to him?" Hazel asked, trying to get her breath. "I don't understand."

Mary shook her head, her eyes dark with grief. "I shouldn't be the one to tell you, Hazel. It's his story to tell."

Hazel felt her heart shatter a little more. "But he won't speak to me, he won't open himself up at all," she replied, wiping her eyes with the back of her hand. "I've tried to talk to him, and we've had a lot of conversations, but I still don't know anything about what's going on in his heart. I thought that if I was the one to begin, if I was the one to show him what it was like to be vulnerable, then he might be more willing to do the same."

Mary gave her a sad smile and patted her hand. "That man's been vulnerable before, and it cut him hard. He's had that hard demeanor ever since. That's what I meant when I told you he wasn't the pleasantest man around these parts, because he's always got that stern face on him. He'd never smile when he came in the store, and over time, he began to visit the town less and less. I reckon he was trying to manage that ranch on his own before admitting he needed someone like you. It got to him, you being there. He doesn't know what to do with that."

Hazel sighed, her heart sinking lower. "Then I can never get through to him. There's no future for us."

"Don't give up hope," Mary said softly, reaching across the table to take Hazel's hand. "I'm sure when you came here, you had plenty of intentions about what your relationship with your husband would be like, and have any of those stuck?"

Shaking her head, Hazel let the truth Mary spoke sink into her soul. She'd come here expecting not to care for her husband, expecting it to just be a firm friendship that would carry on through the years. She'd never thought to feel any kind of affection for him and certainly not love. And now here she was, feeling as though he'd torn her heart from her chest and ripped it apart in front of her, leaving her bleeding and alone.

"Stephen is struggling because his marriage hasn't been what he expected," Mary continued, her gaze firm. "You need to know why that is, but I can't be the one to tell you. The only way the two of you are going to be able to move forward together is if he's the one to open his heart to you."

Hazel's shoulders slumped. "But I don't even know where he is. I could stay at the ranch for days, and he could stay out in the pastures, making sure to avoid me. How am I to speak to him if he won't even come near me?"

Mary paused for a moment, her eyes roving around the small kitchen as she thought. "You're going to have to be stubborn, my dear. Don't give in to his excuses; don't do what he's asking, even if his words hurt. There's pain underneath, a deep, cutting pain that I don't think I'll ever fully understand. He's never spoken a word about it to anyone, not since the day it all came to light." She sighed heavily and shook her head, grimacing. "I know I'm frustrating you even further by not going into detail, but I can't. What I *will* say is that it's maybe a good idea for you to go to the church and speak to the pastor there. Ask to see his register of births, deaths, and marriages. That should give you a starting point. Maybe once you know that, Stephen will be more willing to speak to you."

Hope burst through Hazel's heart as she practically threw herself from the table, enveloping Mary in a hug. Her pain and distress did not go away, but at least now she had somewhere to start. Something she could use to get Stephen to open up to her.

"Thank you, Mary," she whispered, dropping a kiss on her cheek before she hurried away.

16

The church was quiet when Hazel entered, with no one inside. She paused for a moment on the threshold, recalling the day she'd first stepped inside here. The day she'd been married to Stephen Grant.

"Hazel, how good to see you." The pastor came in behind her, an apologetic look on his face. "I'm sorry I'm just getting here—" He came to a sudden stop, frowning heavily. "Whatever's the matter?"

"I need to see your register of births, deaths, and marriages," Hazel said, trying to sound firm and decisive despite the fact that her voice trembled. "Please, I need to see it now."

The pastor shook his head slowly, taking her elbow and guiding her to sit down. "I'm not sure I can do that, Hazel, not without knowing what the problem is."

"Please," Hazel whispered, wondering if her agony would ever cease. "Stephen is making arrangements to send me away, and I don't know why. I don't know what happened to him before, but Mary said to come here and ask you for the register."

The pastor shook his head, a rather grave expression on his face. "I can assure you that unless there has been unfaithfulness of some kind, I will not be making any arrangements to void this marriage, Hazel." His sharp eyes pierced her, and she flushed, shaking her head.

"There has been none of that, I promise," she replied, keeping her gaze as steady as she could. "Was he married before? Is that why he won't let himself love me?"

There was nothing but silence for a few minutes. The pastor pressed his lips together, looking rather frustrated, but said nothing. Hazel waited in both impatience and agony, desperate to know whether or not he would let her see the register.

"I do not have to get the register out, Hazel," he said eventually. "I know all too well the story of your husband's first marriage."

Hazel pressed one hand to her heart, a single tear tracking down her cheek. "So he was married?"

"Yes, he was," the pastor replied quietly. "To a Miss Jessie Miller. It is not for me to go into details but—"

The door suddenly opened behind them. Wiping her eyes free of tears, Hazel turned to see Stephen standing framed in the doorway, his eyes wide with horror.

"Ah, Stephen," the pastor said warmly, as though he had been expecting him. "Your wife is here. I think you had best talk."

Stephen held on to the door, slowly beginning to back away. "No, I don't think I can."

"You are going to stay here and talk to your wife," the pastor replied firmly. "I insist on it. Don't try and back away now, Stephen. I will not give you what you are looking for, for it would be a sin in the eyes of God."

Stephen shook his head, his eyes fixed on the pastor. "I must let her go. This has all been a mistake."

"It would be a mistake if you turned from her now," the

pastor replied softly. "Find your courage. What is kept in your heart should have been shared with your wife long ago."

"Please, Stephen," Hazel said, getting to her feet. "I don't understand any of this. I need to know why you are trying to send me away."

For a long moment, she thought Stephen was about to turn and run away from her, but at the pastor's cajoling, he finally came into the church. Just as he did so, the pastor slipped away, leaving them both alone.

Hazel's vision blurred as Stephen came to sit down across from her. He held his hat in his hands, twisting it back and forth as he looked everywhere but at her face. Lines of pain and confusion were on his face.

Her own heart burned with pain, twisting in much the same way as his hat. She felt as though he held her own heart there in his hands, pulling and stretching it in as many different ways as he could, until she could take no more.

The silence grew deafening. He did not say a single word to her, and she could find nothing to say to him. He *had* to be the one who spoke first. He had to find the willingness to tell her everything.

"Her name was Miss Jessie Miller." His voice was hoarse, cracking with emotion. "I married her four years ago this summer."

"Did you love her?" Hazel asked, her stomach clenching.

Finally, his eyes met hers, but only for a second.

"Yes, I did. Deeply. We had known each other for so long that it was as if we were soulmates. She knew everything about me, and I thought I knew everything about her." He shook his head, his gaze dropping to the floor. "There were the four of us at that time: myself, my best friend Joseph, his girl Clara, and my girl, Jessie."

Hazel swallowed hard, seeing his heart slowly begin to open

in front of her. It was as if the words were being dragged from his lips, each one burning and painful.

"I wanted to marry Jessie for a long time, but it took her a while to come around to the idea," he continued, a distant look in his eyes. "Maybe that should have served as a warning to me, but I couldn't think of that at the time. I just thought she was enjoying the freedom that came with being young and that she wanted to enjoy that for a little longer. My parents, who were alive at the time, thought she was just perfect for me. We talked about marriage for a long time, thinking about the kind of family we'd want to have, where we'd want to settle." Stephen looked up at her, his jaw set. "So, one day, we set the date."

"So you've been in this church before," Hazel whispered, understanding now why he'd been so hesitant when they'd first come to the altar. "You've given your vows before."

He nodded, the hat dropping from his hands as he clenched his hands together. "I sure did. To have and to hold, all of it. And I meant every word. My heart was true, my intentions steadfast. I swore before God that I'd be faithful all the days of my life, and she did the same." He gave a half smile, the regret written plainly on his features. "Her eyes were so clear, her voice so pure. There was no doubt in my mind that we'd be happily married for the rest of our lives."

Unable to stand the pain on his face, Hazel reached out and took one of his hands, running her thumb gently over the back of his hand. "I know something terrible happened. I can see it on your face."

He closed his eyes tightly, as though trying to push away the pain he felt. "I ain't never spoken to anyone about what happened."

"You can tell me," Hazel promised, praying that he would speak to her. "I'm your wife, Stephen. I want to know. I want to understand you."

For a moment, she thought he would tug his hand away and leave the church, telling her that he couldn't do it. He didn't. He took a long, shaky breath and started to speak.

"Around the time we got married, my best friend Joseph called things off with his girl—or she called it off with him. I was never quite sure. Anyway, that meant he spent a lot of time with us. Since we didn't have a place of our own yet, we were living with my parents. It seemed a real nice setup, and everyone got along just fine. What I didn't know was that Joseph was pouring out his troubles to Jessie, and she was taking it all in, listening to him and trying her best to care for him." Grunting, he shook his head. "It's not as though she wasn't willing though. I should have seen it sooner, but I was oblivious to the whole thing. After all, Joseph was my best friend and Jessie was my wife, the one who loved me with her whole heart." Looking up at Hazel, he held her gaze steadily. "Or so I thought."

"Oh, Stephen," Hazel breathed, her heart rending for him. "They didn't."

"I don't' know where they are now," he replied hoarsely, dropping his head. "I found them one day when I came home unexpectedly. I was so shocked with what I'd seen that I spent the night out on the plains, riding into the darkness in an effort to control my pain." He swallowed hard, no longer able to look at her. "When I came back to town, they were both gone."

Hazel did not know what to say, aware that his pain was still raw. He'd been hiding it, carrying it alone for so long that it had never had a chance to heal. There had been no one for him to turn to, no one for him to share his grief with.

"My parents died of a feverish illness only a few months later," he muttered, dashing a hand across his eyes. "It took me a long time to get myself back together. That was when I decided to buy the ranch and start over."

Hazel pressed his hand. "And the pastor granted you a divorce?"

He nodded. "That was the only letter I ever got from her. An address of where to send the papers. The day I got them back, I spent an hour or more just looking at them, realizing how much of my world had come to a swift end. I didn't know how to begin again, how to get rid of the pain in my heart. And so, I bottled it all up and kept it inside. I've never spoken to anyone about this, and I vowed I never would." He lifted his eyes to hers, regret filling them. "I guess I've broken that vow."

"But I won't break mine," Hazel replied, placing her other hand on top of his. "Stephen, why did you try to push me away after what we shared last night?"

He sighed and dropped his head, slowly pulling his hand away from hers. "Love is too risky. I can't let myself go through that again."

The loss of his hand in hers brought such a stab of pain, Hazel was forced to catch her breath for a moment.

"You deserve better than this hollow shell," Stephen finished, getting to his feet. "I really think this is for the best."

In a moment, Hazel was in front of him, blocking his path to the door of the church. "I think I can decide for myself what's best for me, Stephen Grant," she said firmly, putting one hand on his chest. "And when have you ever known me just to do what you want, when you want?"

He shook his head, no smile on his face. "I can't do this, Hazel."

"Why not? Because you're afraid that I'll do the same as Jessie did? That I'll find someone better and run away with them?"

The look in his eyes told her that was exactly the case.

"That's why you wanted a marriage without love or affection," Hazel said aloud, reaching her hand up to touch his face gently. "Believe me, I thought I wanted that too, but look how that's changed."

"I should never have kissed you last night," he said, turning a little way from her so that she was forced to drop her hand. "That was a mistake."

Hazel shook her head and smiled, realizing that she now understood her husband better than she had ever before. "You kissed me because you felt something for me, didn't you?"

She caught his hands when he didn't answer, looking intently into his face.

"Don't be afraid to tell me the truth, Stephen," she said softly. "I need to know how you feel."

He closed his eyes and nodded, as though ashamed of what he felt. "I've started to be happy again," he said, as though confessing some terrible sin. "The way you've spoken to me, pushed me into things I'd never normally do, that was horrible for a while. But, slowly, I've come to appreciate that."

She pressed his hand. "You've still never come paddling in the creek with me."

He let out a bark of laughter despite himself, running a hand over his eyes. "I know."

"When I first came here, I was determined never to love another man again," Hazel said, stepping closer to him. "I had closed up my heart, glad that I was entering into a marriage that wouldn't ask for any of my emotions. I didn't want to trust you, I wanted to only rely on myself. I pushed back when you tried to take away my freedom, refusing to do anything you asked so as to prove to you that I wasn't the timid, quiet little wife you wanted. After what Christopher did, I was determined not to be pushed around."

"And you sure proved that," he murmured, finally turning back towards her.

"Slowly, I began to trust you," Hazel continued softly. "I realized that you were nothing like Christopher, that I could trust you never to force yourself—or your demands on me in the way he did. And so, because I began to trust you, my heart slowly began to heal. When you kissed me last night, it was because your heart is beginning to heal from the pain it has suffered, beginning to be open to trusting again, to *loving* again. And instead of accepting it, you ran from it. You ran from me."

There was a moment of silence, a moment where he looked into her eyes and his expression softened.

"I know that I love you, Stephen," Hazel whispered, putting one hand flat on his chest. "You're right that it always comes with a risk, but it's a risk I'm willing to take. I believed you when you said you'll never hit me, never force yourself on me. I know you —not as much as I'd like to—but enough to know that you're a man of your word. Your kindness in giving me Daisy, your willingness to begin to do things outside of the way you'd rather do things, they all show me the man of integrity you are." She pressed her hand to his cheek, her eyes bright with tears. "How could I not love you?"

Stephen looked at her steadily, taking in all that she had said. Then, with a groan, he closed his eyes and leaned into her hand, his shoulders slumping.

"I'm too ashamed to tell you that I'm afraid," he said eventually, his eyes still firmly closed. "I'm afraid to let you in my heart. I've been fighting it for weeks, but the very thing I don't want has refused to leave me. Instead, it has grown into something huge, something I'm afraid to acknowledge."

Hazel said nothing, waiting for him to speak. There was so much in his heart, so much to be said, that she needed to give him the space to do it.

"I don't want to be apart from you," he finally admitted, opening his eyes and looking down at her. "Oh, Hazel, I don't want you to go."

She laughed softly, putting her arms around his neck. "Stephen, I don't want to leave you either. I wasn't planning on just packing up my things and taking the train back home just because you decided things were over."

He rested his forehead against hers, his breath tickling her cheek. "Can you take this broken man, Hazel? I've got so much to tell you, so much to talk to you about, but my heart is still learning what it means to live without pain, without doubt."

The lump in her throat was so great that she could hardly speak. "We're both broken," she replied tenderly. "But do you think you can trust me, Stephen? Can you open your heart to me and let me in?"

His lips touched hers for the briefest kiss, and Hazel felt tears dampen her cheeks.

"I know I can," he murmured, his arms now around her waist. "I'm sorry for what I did, Hazel. I won't turn from you again. I won't be afraid to say I love you."

Those words entered her heart and stayed there, happiness running all through her. "And I love you, Stephen. For as long as we both shall live."

～

THE END

LOVE LIGHT FAITH

Receive a FREE inspirational romance eBook by visiting our website and signing up for our mailing list. Click the link or enter www.LoveLightFaith.com into your browser.

The newsletter will also provide information on upcoming books and special offers.

THANK YOU

Thank you for reading this book! Avid readers like you make an author's world shine.

If you've enjoyed this book, or any other books by Ruby Hill, please don't hesitate to review them on Amazon or Goodreads. Every single review makes an incredible difference. The reason for this is simple: other readers trust reviews more than professional endorsements. For this reason, we rely on our readers to spread the good word.

Sending you endless appreciation, plus a little love, light and faith!

OTHER STORIES YOU WILL LOVE

If you loved reading this book, discover other heartwarming romance stories you'll love. All books are stand-alone stories and can be read in any order.

Mail Order Bride

Finding Hope
A mail order bride is left at the train station by her betrothed. Alone and afraid, Grace is offered a second chance at happiness.

Regency Books

An Earl's Agreement
An arranged marriage turns dangerous when he will stop at nothing to make her his bride! Will her hero prevail?

Married to a Marquess
After her wedding day, Alice never saw her husband again. She must now take charge of her own life if she is to ever know happiness!

A Viscount's Second Chance
Henry is thrilled to have a second chance at love, but he risks losing Eleanor again when a scandal threatens to tear them apart!

A Duke for Christmas
Isabella did not want to end up on Charles' doorstep, but it might be exactly what both of them need... A clean, Regency romance to warm your heart.

Unexpected Earl
Catherine is enamored with Lord Kerr and plans to marry him, but Lord Linton will do all he can to stop the union.

Printed in Great Britain
by Amazon

36470830R00076